THE
END
OF US

USA TODAY BESTSELLING AUTHOR
KENNEDY FOX

LOVE IN ISOLATION SERIES READING ORDER

The Two of Us
Elijah & Cameron
A brother's best friend, forced proximity romance

The Best of Us
Ryan & Kendall
A best friend's brother, snowed-in together romance

The End of Us
Tristan & Piper
A bodyguard, age gap, forced proximity romance

The Heart of Us
Easton & Tatum
A reverse age gap, close proximity romance

The Fall of Us
Finn & Oakley
An enemies to lovers, close proximity romance

The Joy of Us
Levi & Fallon
A reverse grumpy / sunshine, close proximity romance

One look at you
My whole life falls in line
I prayed for you
Before I called you mine
Oh, I can't believe it's true sometimes
Oh, I can't believe it's true
I get to love you
It's the best thing that I'll ever do

"I Get to Love You"
-Lyndsey Elm

CHAPTER ONE

PIPER

THIS EVENING, my sister, Kendall, married the love of her life, Ryan St. James. The ceremony was gorgeous, and their sweet vows reminded me of how painfully single I am. When they finally kissed, tears trailed down my cheeks, and there wasn't a dry eye in the room.

After posing for the photographer, the wedding party's escorted to the reception hall that's filled with guests. My parents, who are considered Manhattan royalty, invited their elite friends and business acquaintances. Ryan's family is in the same circle, so anyone who's anybody is in attendance tonight. It's one of the many reasons it looks like the Secret Service is guarding the place.

I smooth my hand across the silk of my bridesmaid dress after I grab a glass of champagne. My sister's best friend, Cami, who's also Ryan's sister, waits in line behind me with her husband, Eli.

"Wasn't the wedding beautiful?" Cami says before I walk away with my glass. She's always been so sweet to me.

"Yes, it's exactly how Kendall always dreamed. Lavish and perfect. Hey, Eli!"

He grins at me, but before we can chat any longer, they're both dragged away by Mrs. St. James. I'm ready to take off these heels and walk around barefoot, but I ignore the pain. Eventually, Kendall and Ryan enter, and I try to scream the loudest for them. The smile on my sister's face is contagious, and I love how happy she is dancing with her new hubby. I order another glass of champagne, then stand off to the side and watch as they're swarmed by people wanting to personally congratulate them.

When I look over my shoulder, I see Tristan, my bodyguard, acting as my shadow while his eyes scan over the crowd. Having him always close is not something I've gotten used to over the past six months. I'm not sure if I ever will.

My parents found it necessary because of who I am—a Montgomery—and because I'm an influential lifestyle vlogger. I've tried to explain parasocial relationships to my mother several times and how it's natural and normal, but she doesn't listen or understand. With over twenty million subscribers to my channel, I'm bound to have crazy people stalk me, but lately, it's gone to a level that even I'm not comfortable with. It's the *only* reason I agreed to have protection with me. Tristan takes his job very seriously. Almost too much.

Since last year, I've been receiving death threats and disgusting email love letters from this guy named Jack, something I've mostly kept to myself. If I pretend it's not happening, I can almost convince myself everything is normal. So that's what I do.

The reception hall is gorgeous with crystal chandeliers and candlelight. As dinner is served, I sit with my parents in the front. My mother has been giddy ever since Kendall told her she was engaged, but right now, I think she's just tipsy. The lobster and scallions nearly melt in my mouth, and I have to stop myself from getting seconds. After dinner, the speeches happen, and the dancing commences.

Once Kendall and Ryan are finally alone, I take my opportunity to bombard them. As soon as I'm close, I squeeze them as tight as I can.

"Everything has been perfect," I say, adoring how great they are together. "Look at you two. Gah, I can't wait to find love like this."

My sister snorts. "It wasn't all butterflies and rainbows, but it was worth it."

I think back to everything they went through to get here. Ryan and Kendall were sent to stock up and decorate the St. James' cabin for her best friend, Cami. The next thing they knew, a freak blizzard blew in, and they were stranded together until the roads were cleared. She's told me how magical the whole experience was, and honestly, it sounds like the plot of a Hallmark movie. With lots of sex between.

Ryan looks over my shoulder. "Who's that?"

I turn to see who he's referring to. "Oh him? It's my bodyguard, Tristan," I explain, keeping the details to myself of why I have a security detail. Kendall knows the basics, but I didn't tell her everything either. She worries enough about me already. The paparazzi and gossip news sites haven't done me any favors over the years. Having a bodyguard again reminds me of high school and how we had a security team anytime we left the house. Once I graduated, I told my dad I could handle myself, but since the threats began, Dad insisted on hiring someone. I didn't argue, though I've been wondering how long he'll make me have one—forever, if it were up to him.

3

"She's kinda a big deal," Kendall tells him with a laugh. "My famous sister."

"Famous? Pfft." I quickly change the subject because today isn't about me. "Before I forget, I think we should have a celebration shot! What would you two like?"

"Anything," Kendall cheerfully says.

Ryan grins. "Surprise us."

"Shoulda never told me that. I'll be right back." I shake my head, then shoot them a smirk.

I rush to the bar, passing the cake on the way. It's a sugary statue-like masterpiece with blinking LED lights and edible flowers. I order our drinks, then carefully carry them back, trying not to spill a drop. I almost ask Tristan to give me a hand, but he's made it very clear to pretend he's not there, so I do.

"So when are we cutting the cake? That thing is gigantic. I don't think I've ever seen one that tall before. It has lights, Kendall. I mean, I saw the picture you texted me, but it literally didn't do it any justice. I'm surprised it's not surrounded by a moat of champagne." I snicker.

"That would've been a good idea, though," she admits as I hand over the glasses. "I almost thought about getting one with diamonds and gold, but Ryan would've lost his shit on me."

"We don't need to eat a multimillion-dollar cake. It all comes out the same, if you know what I mean," he tells me, and I can't help but laugh as Kendall playfully rolls her eyes. One thing I love about Ryan is even though his family is filthy rich, he doesn't act like it. He's mindful of how money's spent and doesn't depend on his parents. It was important for him to have his own career outside of the St. James name.

Ryan looks at the shot and smells it. "What is this?"

I start chuckling before I can get it out. "It's called Death by Sex. 'Cause I'm sure that will be you two later tonight."

"God, I hope so," Kendall admits, biting her lower lip and meeting Ryan's eyes.

I hold up my glass and they join in. "To the happy couple! So excited you're finally getting your happily ever afters."

We shoot them down, and Kendall seems shocked by the taste, and I know it's because they don't burn like most shots.

"So when are we finally cutting that giant-ass cake?" I ask again as my sister goes over the itinerary with me one more time. Just as my aunt Mildred walks up, I take it as my opportunity to excuse myself. The last thing I want to do is start answering questions about my career or when I plan to get married. I have a lot of things on my bucket list to check off before I'll think about settling down.

Tristan moves in close to me as I make my way through the crowd. He places his hand on my back and guides me around as he watches our surroundings. Although he doesn't really say much to me, and holding a solid conversation with him is impossible, I appreciate his company. Having him near eases my mind.

Right on schedule with the super-strict itinerary, Kendall and Ryan cut the cake. He places a little chunk in her mouth while she smears frosting on his face. Then she stands on her tiptoes to lick it off. I pull out my camera just in time to video it because I might share a few clips with my followers.

"Do you want a slice?" I ask Tristan, and he shakes his head.

"Damn, you're missing out. It's *orgasmic*," I say, going for a second one. I think I see a smirk play on his lips, but then he goes back to his stoic self.

After the music starts again, I decide to sit at one of the

high tops that faces the dance floor. My feet are killing me, but that's what I get. I talk to a few family friends and decide I need another shot after being asked when I'm gonna get hitched and pop out babies. As I make my way across the room, a man with a crazed look in his eyes approaches me.

He grabs my wrists with a tight grip and forcefully jerks me forward. "What are you doing?" I scream, nearly losing my balance. His nails dig into my skin, and he's holding me so tight I can't get away.

"You're mine, bitch," the man says, and that's when I realize it's my stalker—Jack. Tristan slams into him with all his weight, and Jack falls into a table, knocking it over. The music stops, and people scream when Tristan pulls a gun from his holster. The crowd rushes around us toward the exit, and security moves in. Someone crashes into Tristan, and he stumbles to the ground. The pistol slides across the floor. I try to help him up, but he's already on his feet. When I look over, Jack's gone.

He disappeared in the commotion.

"Where the fuck did he go?" Tristan hisses.

"I don't know," I breathlessly say as he pulls me close and escorts me outside. He's talking to someone in code on the earpiece, and his jaw locks tight when he's done. Adrenaline floods me, and I'm wobbly on my feet. Unfortunately, we're not the only ones leaving.

I turn around, not seeing my parents or sister, knowing that Kendall's reception is in utter chaos and it's all my fault.

"What are we doing?" I ask as he keeps a firm grip on me.

"We need to leave immediately," he grits out, escorting me to a car parked in the front. There's a driver inside, and I wonder if Tristan had an escape plan just in case. I climb in, and he's beside me with his gun in hand.

"To my hotel, then her apartment," he demands, and we head toward the city.

"How'd he find me?" My wrists hurt from how hard I was grabbed.

I unlock my phone, and Tristan turns to me.

"Jack tracked you through that." He glares at it. "The fact that he got into the venue shows he's smarter than any of us realized, especially with the added security."

"I know. It was frightening. Can I call my parents?"

"They know I have you and that we're getting out of New York. He's hacked his way inside your device, and I don't know what information he's gotten."

He grabs my cell and holds it in his firm grip.

I glare at him. "I can't be without my phone."

"I'll get you a burner."

"What's that?"

"A replacement, one he doesn't know about."

I'm trying not to cry, feeling so vulnerable and exposed to an obsessed fan turned maniac. No telling what pictures, videos, and messages of mine he's seen, and the fact that Jack tracked my location is even scarier.

"Can I at least pack my things?" I ask, realizing he just said we're leaving New York.

"You'll have fifteen minutes when we get to your apartment, and that's it. Bring enough to keep you dressed while we're in hiding."

Hiding? I try not to freak out and suck in deep breaths to help me calm down, but it doesn't work. My phone buzzes, and Tristan looks down at it. There's a preview from Kendall.

"You can reply to your sister, just this once, but don't give her any specifics," he says, handing it over.

I unlock it and hurry and read what she sent.

Kendall: Mom and Dad told me what happened. Please tell me you're safe.

I immediately reply.

Piper: I'm with Tristan. I have to be careful what I say until I get a burner phone, but we're going into hiding. I'll be safe with him and will text you as soon as I can. I'm so sorry this happened on your special night. I love you guys!

Kendall: It's not your fault. I love you too! Text me and keep me updated when you're able to, please!

Relief floods through me, knowing she's not mad. She's waited her whole life for this wedding.

Piper: I will. Plus, it might not be so bad being locked up with my hot bodyguard ;)

Kendall: Don't say I didn't warn you before...don't get involved!

Piper: You're no fun!

Kendall: Love you, sis. Please stay safe.

Tristan takes my phone before I can say anything else and turns it off.

"What the hell? I didn't get to tell my sister I love her back."

His green eyes meet mine. "She knows. We can't risk anything else."

I swallow hard, pissed. I don't say a word the rest of the way.

We stop at the hotel where Tristan has been staying while working for my parents. It's two blocks away from my apartment.

Before he gets out, he turns to me. "Stay inside this car. I'll be right back."

He rushes inside, and I take a quick moment to let my emotions out. The driver doesn't make eye contact and pretends I'm invisible. The tears fall because I feel helpless. Running for my life wasn't on my list of things to do today.

Tristan returns carrying a black duffel bag. He searches up and down the sidewalk before he opens the door, then we drive a few blocks over.

When we finally make it to my apartment, the place is surrounded by paparazzi.

"Fuck," Tristan groans, and this time, I agree with his sentiments. While I usually don't mind the photographers and use the paps as much as they use me, I could live without them right now. "Make it ten minutes," Tristan mutters as he swings open the door. He forces his way through the crowd, guiding me up the stoop of my building. The flashes are blinding, and handfuls of people are screaming my name. It's too much as I'm internally panicking.

Before he lets me in, Tristan checks every room with his gun drawn. My mind races a million miles per minute as I grab all of my vlogging gear, laptop, memory cards, and chargers. In the distance, Tristan's talking on the phone to someone. When he gives me a five-minute warning, I let out an annoyed breath. Knowing I need clothes, I grab random things from my closet and dresser drawers along with my travel cosmetic bag.

"We gotta get going," Tristan snaps, entering my bedroom just as I zip my suitcase. He lifts it along with my backpack. I take one last look at my apartment, then we lock up. In that short amount of time, the paps have doubled.

"Back the fuck off. You're in the way," Tristan grits out, making a path for me. My heart is galloping by the time we get into the car and speed off.

Tristan turns, noticing the entourage of vehicles chasing us. "Of course."

I wish I could sink into the seat and disappear. "They're relentless."

"Once we arrive at the private airport, they'll be stopped."

I glance over at him. "We're getting on a plane?"

"Yeah."

"They're going to know we're flying somewhere."

He meets my eyes. "They won't know where we're going, and neither will you."

"Why not?"

"The less you know, the better."

I clench my jaw, angry that he's not giving me any details. We zoom through the private gate, and those following us are left behind at the security entrance. The car pulls up to my parents' private jet. Within minutes, my bags are being loaded, and we've boarded. After we're buckled, the plane taxis to the runway. Once we take off, I pull out my laptop, and before I can log in with my fingerprint, Tristan slams it shut.

"No internet. *At all.* Jack tracked your phone, and I don't know if that's infected too. As soon as you connect to the internet, your IP can be tracked."

My nostrils flare. "Do you have any idea how many

rumors are going to be started about me? Everyone will know I fled from my sister's wedding, packed my shit, and escaped on a plane."

"I don't give two shits," he firmly states.

"Of course you don't," I snap. He doesn't realize how hard I've worked to stay out of the drama.

I grab my AirPods, then realize I don't have my phone to listen to music, so I put them back into their case. Closing my eyes, I think back to all the meet & greets, public appearances, and videos that got me into this mess.

While it's not Tristan's fault that this happened, he seems to have zero compassion for me. Not that I want his sympathy, but my everyday life involves the internet, so dealing with all of this on top of having all access ripped away in a blink is a lot at once.

My mind reels, and I try to fall asleep, but the thoughts come and go so fast that I grow anxious instead of tired. I look down at the silk dress I'm still wearing and am reminded how quickly everything happened and how lucky I am to be safe. I already wish this nightmare would end, and it literally just started.

CHAPTER TWO

TRISTAN

I KNOW PIPER'S PISSED, but there's nothing I can do about it. She's used to always getting her way, and considering she was born with a silver spoon in her mouth, it's not hard to guess why. However, I take my missions seriously, especially when her life is on the line. When we're an hour outside of our destination, I connect to the Wi-Fi on the plane and text my brother. He immediately responds.

Tristan: Hey, I'll be in town tonight.

Easton: Is everything okay? Did something happen?

Tristan: I'll explain everything tomorrow. Is there any way you can help stock the beach house with food? I don't know how long we'll be staying.

Easton: We?

Tristan: Yeah.

When he realizes I'm not going to give any more details, he sends another message.

Easton: I can be there in the morning before my shift.

Tristan: Appreciate it.

I lock my phone, knowing I'll eventually have to fill him in. It's not something I'm looking forward to, considering the impending danger that follows being someone like Piper Montgomery's bodyguard. My family worries about my well-being often, and that's the last thing I want. It's taken years for my parents to stop hounding me about staying safe, and once this is splashed on the news, concern will follow. My mother worried when I was in the military, and I think after everything that has happened, she always will.

Three and a half hours later, the plane touches down.

I've gotten the silent treatment during the entire flight, and I don't know if she realizes or not, but it doesn't bother me. Honestly, I'd rather her be quiet than hear her whining about her first-world problems. There are bigger issues than her not being able to log on to the internet, but I'll never be able to convince her otherwise.

Once the plane comes to a stop, the cabin lights turn on, and the pilots wish us well. A concierge is waiting by the rental car her parents set up, and I quickly sign the paperwork, then place Piper's belongings in the back seat. The humidity is the first thing I notice, and it's something I haven't missed living in New York.

"Jesus, it's hot," Piper complains, smoothing her hair away from her face.

I get inside the vehicle and am happy the windows are

tinted dark. Although it's right after two o'clock in the morning, and I doubt anyone is searching for Piper here, I can never be too cautious.

Piper puts on her seat belt and stares out the window as we leave. I turn onto the main road, and her eyes are glued outside.

"Palm trees? Are we in Florida?"

Smirking, I increase my speed onto the freeway without responding. She huffs and doesn't say anything else.

I could drive to my family's beach house with my eyes closed. Though I wish I were visiting under different circumstances, I'll take what I can get.

Glancing over at her, I notice she's fallen asleep. Though she's a huge YouTube star with millions of adoring fans, death threats from a pervert had never happened before now. It's actually shocking it took this long, considering how obsessed people are with her.

But Jack? He's taken it to the extreme.

I turn onto a small paved road, then pull into the driveway. Luckily, the doors are equipped with security keypads, so I only need a code to enter. I put the car in park and lightly nudge her.

Piper wakes and looks around. "We're here?"

"Yeah. I'll grab your things."

She nods, and we get out of the car. I swing her backpack over my shoulders then grab my duffel and her suitcase. When we walk in, I realize the cabin hasn't been aired out and smells musty.

Piper looks disgusted. "What is this place?"

"It's my family's beach house."

"Wait, there's a beach?"

I nod and point at the windows, though she won't be able

to see since it's dark. "It's private access, and during the day, you can see it from here."

"So we *are* in Florida, aren't we?"

"Yes. But that's all I can share. It's better if you don't know exactly where we are."

She swallows hard. "Do my parents know we've arrived?"

"I'll call your dad once you're settled, but he was notified via text that we landed and picked up the car."

"Okay," she tells me as her eyes scan over the place. I wish I could read her mind. This house is far from the luxury she's used to.

She makes her way into the living room, then glances at the small kitchen and moves closer to the large wall of windows. Since the moon isn't out, seeing the water is impossible. I open the windows, allowing the natural breeze to flow in.

"Your room is upstairs." I lead the way. Once on the second floor, I turn to where she'll be staying and wheel her suitcase inside.

"Where's the master bedroom?" She walks inside, noticing it's not large.

"There isn't one," I explain. "I'll be right next door. It'll allow me to be closer."

The look on her face is nothing short of horrified, and I try not to laugh.

"This is a joke, right?" She's seething.

"Let me set something straight before you start complaining—you're not here for a vacation. I know you think you're roughing it, but try to be respectful."

She glares at me, then takes her suitcase and throws it on the bed to unzip it. "Where's the bathroom?"

"Down the hall."

"There's only one?"

I meet her eyes. "Upstairs, yes, which means we'll be sharing. Lucky you."

Piper shakes her head and grabs some clothes. Storming past me, she finds it, then slams the door shut. The toilet flushes, then the water turns on for a while before finally shutting off. Five more minutes pass before she comes out with her hair up in a bun.

"Can you turn on the air conditioner? I'm sweating."

I chuckle and walk to the large rectangle windows and open them. "There you go. Nature's A/C."

"You're shitting me." She looks like she's about to explode. "Wait until my dad hears about this."

"He's aware. Said it would be good character development for you."

Her lips move into a firm straight line. "I hate *everything* about this. A small room and bed. No central air-conditioning, and it stinks like a wet dog."

I ignore her comments. "Now that you've gotten that out of your system, it's time for some ground rules."

Piper glares like she's ready to murder me.

"The house does have internet."

She perks up.

"But…"

"I knew you weren't done."

I cross my arms over my chest and lean against the doorframe. "Under no circumstances can you connect to it."

"Of course I can't."

"You also can't check your social media," I add.

"Without the internet, it's impossible. Can I at least have my cell back? You can put it on airplane mode if it makes you feel better."

I shake my head. "I don't know what Jack has access to at

this point, and I'm not willing to risk it. If you log in from a different device, he might have your socials hacked. The last thing you want is him showing up, trust me."

She sighs.

"You *can* use your laptop without the internet though. So if you have work that you can do without being online, feel free."

"I have sponsored videos and pictures I need to edit, but it's not like I can post them. All of this…" She looks around, then meets my eyes. "Is what my nightmares are made from."

"You're being dramatic."

"And you're being an ass," she snaps.

"Not the first time I've been called that."

"For the past six months, you've barely said anything to me and now you're barking orders at me. I kinda liked you better when you didn't talk." She zips up her suitcase and places it on the floor, then looks at me. "You're dismissed."

I roll my eyes regardless of how disrespectful she's being. Right now, she's acting like a spoiled little brat who's not getting her way, and I'm two seconds from telling her as much. Instead of speaking my mind, I walk away. It's easier considering I have no idea how long we'll be stuck in this beach house together.

When I enter my room, she slams her door shut. I take my guns out of the chest holster and set them on the nightstand. Unzipping my duffel, I pull out the ammo that I packed along with my clothes, then call Mr. Montgomery.

"Thanks for the updates as you traveled," he says.

"No problem. We've made it to our destination without any issues."

There's silence for a moment. "How's Piper? She understands the rules?"

"Yes, she's been made aware. Also, she's *very* pissed."

Mr. Montgomery chuckles. "I figured as much. Anyway, I have a few people trying to track down this man. I'll let you know what we find out."

"Sounds good."

"Please keep my daughter safe, Tristan."

"I pledged my life to protect this country, and I take my duty of keeping Piper safe just as seriously, sir."

"Appreciate that. I'll stay in touch."

After the call ends, I change clothes and replay everything that happened tonight. If Jack would've had a gun or a knife, he could've easily hurt Piper or someone else. The fact that he chose a very intimate setting to pull this is psychotic, almost as if he wanted the attention it would bring. Maybe he did.

Instead of climbing in bed, I go downstairs and check every door and window to make sure they're secure.

Piper may be a twenty-one-year-old brat, but she doesn't deserve this. While I don't completely understand her life as an influencer and probably never will, I respect her work ethic and how determined she is to be successful.

She doesn't need a job considering how wealthy her family is, but she chooses to record, edit, and post videos almost daily. Over the past few years she's made a name for herself and has become an internet sensation. The girl has her own merchandise and sayings trademarked. She's appeared on TV shows, been a featured guest on celebrity podcasts, and gets paid to attend birthday parties for the elite. Companies send her ridiculous amounts of free products with the hopes that she'll mention it on her channel or in her Instagram stories. I've never seen anything like this in my life. Most of it flies over my head.

My job is to keep her out of trouble, protect her from

psychos, and make sure she doesn't get herself in dangerous situations. She's not aware of her surroundings most of the time, and feels safe on the streets of New York when she shouldn't. Piper's a pretty girl, very recognizable, has a cult following, and views the world through rose-colored glasses. Meanwhile, I'm jaded with trust issues wrapped in PTSD.

I have a feeling Jack won't be the last person who tries to attack her. Piper's just too naive to realize it.

CHAPTER THREE

PIPER

DAY 1

THE MOMENT I WAKE UP, dread rolls through me. I slept like garbage for many reasons, but mostly because of the cheap scratchy sheets on this lumpy bed. Not to mention, I'm covered in sweat. If all of that wasn't bad enough, I feel like bugs are crawling on me from the windows being open all night.

I'm living in a literal hell.

I head to the bathroom and scrub my face, then readjust my bun. Since I only grabbed what could fit in my carry-on, I don't have my normal essentials. If Tristan doesn't find a way for me to get the things I need, I'll cry. Wearing only a thin pair of shorts and a T-shirt, I grab my camera, then head downstairs. I hope there's good news waiting for me. If my stalker's been caught, that means we can leave, and I can go back to my comfy air-conditioned apartment. But I'm not holding my breath.

"Morning," Tristan says shirtless, but doesn't turn around.

His back is sweaty as if he'd been working out. He's at the stove cooking, which means we must have groceries now.

"Hello," another man's voice says, catching me off guard and making me jump. "Sorry, didn't mean to scare you." He's a younger version of Tristan.

Tristan spins around with a skillet of eggs. "This is my brother, Easton. He went to the store for us."

"Nice to meet you," I say. "I didn't know you were coming, or I would've made a list."

Easton glances at Tristan, who's watching us, and gives him a shrug.

"I'm going to need some things if we're staying here a while. When will you be back?"

Easton straightens in the chair and flashes an amused smirk. "I don't work for you."

His words are a slap in the face. Tristan stifles a laugh when I glare at him.

"Then why are you here?" I snap, crossing my arms over my chest.

"Sit and eat. You can give me your list later," Tristan orders, setting a plate on the breakfast bar. "He lives forty-five minutes away, so he'll return when he's able."

I stare at the burnt bacon and dry eggs sprinkled with pepper and frown. I fight the urge to throw up. "This looks like dog food."

Easton snorts as Tristan furrows his brows.

"I'm not a personal chef, so eat it or starve. I don't care either way."

Tristan sits across from Easton and they begin to eat. Deciding to join them, I take mine and plop down at the end of the table.

"So, are you a bodyguard too?" I ask Easton.

"No, I own a shop in town called Belvedere's Surf & Suits. I live in the apartment above it."

"Really? Can you bring me a swimsuit when you return? I wasn't able to bring one with me, and if I'm stuck here, I might as well get a tan."

"You're not going on the beach," Tristan barks.

"What? It's right there. You're going to keep me from getting some vitamin D?"

"Take a multivitamin if you're that concerned."

I roll my eyes, stabbing my fork into the eggs. "Why? It's literally thirty seconds from the house."

"Same reason I can't be seen. Your stalker knows what I look like. I can't risk someone recognizing either of us."

"So, we're both stuck inside this house for God knows how long?"

"Correct. It's why Easton will shop for us."

"Well, I'm gonna guess Easton didn't get tampons…" I blurt out.

Easton chokes on his orange juice. Tristan shakes his head and speaks up. "Add it to your list then."

I turn to his brother. "Do you need pictures or will you be able to find the correct ones?"

The corner of his lips tilt up as he wipes juice off his chin. "I have mostly women employees and have dated in the past, so yeah, I think I can figure out super versus regular. Or are you a wings girl?"

I glower at his snarky comment, then flash a cheeky grin. "Only on my heavy days when I'm a real delight to be around. Isn't that right, Tristan?" I hope to get a reaction out of him because he acts like a robot otherwise.

Easton barks out a laugh, his face filled with amusement.

"You have your hands full, brother. I'm only sorry I didn't bring you a case of beer."

Tristan kicks him under the table and we stare him down, but for different reasons.

"I'm the one who'll need alcohol. Tristan's dry sense of humor might bore me to death," I groan, although I could get used to waking up to the view of his six-pack abs and muscular arms. The eye candy *almost* makes up for his lack of personality.

I scarf down the eggs just to get something in my stomach. "They taste better than they look," I tell Tristan. "Next time, less pepper and add cheese."

"I told you they needed something else," Easton gloats, pointing his fork at Tristan. "But you said she was lactose intolerant."

I blink, jerking my head toward Tristan. "How did you know that?"

"So you are?" Easton asks.

"Yeah, but I can still eat small amounts of dairy," I admit.

"Any other requests?" Tristan deadpans.

"Let me go home," I blurt out with a flicker of hope.

"Since we've been here less than twenty-four hours, you might want to spread out your complaints or you'll run out of things to whine about," Tristan says without an ounce of emotion.

"As much as I'd love to stay and hang out, I have to get to work." Easton stands, then sets his plate in the sink. "I'll try to return this weekend. Think you can last that long?" he sarcastically asks me.

I cross my arms. "Let's hope Mother Nature gets on your schedule. It's bad enough I'm sweating like a hippo."

Easton nods at Tristan as if to say *good luck*.

"I'll text you," Tristan tells him before Easton leaves.

I set my half-eaten breakfast on the counter, then open the fridge. It's filled with the essentials: milk, butter, cheese, and yogurt. But not the Greek yogurt I prefer. I notice there are no protein shakes either. I check the freezer and find frozen pizzas and waffles. In the pantry, there are boxes of pasta, marinara sauce, bread, and a box of cereal.

"You got us bachelor food," I tell Tristan. "Where are the fruit and veggies?"

"I thought it was more important to have food that'd last longer than a few days since I didn't know when he'd have time to drop by again."

"Can't we have groceries delivered?" I ask, staring at the unappetizing options.

"No."

I groan, shutting the pantry door and reaching for my camera. Though I'm not as presentable as I normally am, it's fitting for the vlog. While I can't upload anything, I can film some content for when I'm allowed to post again.

Smiling wide, I hit the record button. "Hey, guys! Welcome back to my channel, or welcome if you're new here. Today I'm giving you the grand tour of the super rustic and cute beach house I'm staying in. I'm not sure when this video will be posted, hopefully really soon, but I just couldn't wait to take you around. So let's start with the charming kitchen and dinette. There's not a lot of food yet, but we just got here, so we'll stock up soon. In the dining room, there's this antique table, and with all the windows, it brings in a ton of natural light, which of course you know I love."

Tristan's staring at me like he wants to comment on

everything I'm saying. Even though I'm making everything out to be fine, we both know it's not. My subscribers don't want to see some rich girl complaining about slumming it, so I keep things cheerful and optimistic. That's a part of my brand and what they're used to seeing. Being Ms. Positivity, who loves life, is what they know me as.

Next, I walk around to the living room and show off the views of the ocean and palm trees. It really is beautiful outside, which is why I wish I was *allowed* to go out there.

After I show the downstairs area, I move to my bedroom. I emphasize how it's charming and quaint, and how fresh air flows through the windows upstairs. It's nothing like my luxury high rise apartment or anywhere I'd willingly stay, but I can't complain when my parents demanded Tristan take me somewhere off-grid. There are neighboring homes, but they're quite a distance away. The property is surrounded by palm trees and the only open space is on the private beach.

But apparently I won't be seeing that anytime soon.

I smile wide and act like I'm having the time of my life. When this is over, I'll put a video together explaining why I was hiding out and put the inevitable rumors to rest. I can only imagine what people will think when they hear there was drama at my sister's wedding and how I escaped then suddenly vanished.

"Are you done filming?" Tristan asks when I walk into the living room. He's showered and changed now, covering all of his sex appeal.

"For now," I say, plopping down on the chair.

"Will you be doing that every day?"

"Doing what?" I sneer, grabbing the remote.

"Pretending you love everything when moments before

you were complaining about the food and whining about no air-conditioning?"

"You wouldn't understand."

I turn on the TV, praying there's cable.

"Understand what exactly?" he asks.

"My life. Sharing things with the public for them to nitpick every single detail. Keeping up appearances," I ramble off only a few things that most people wouldn't get.

"Then why do you do it? Why put your life on display like that if you're just going to fake it? Not like you need the extra attention. Everyone already knows who your family is."

I snap my gaze to him. "I don't *fake* it, I just don't emphasize the shitty moments. And I film because of what's known about my family. I want to prove every single tabloid wrong and show them who I am, not just what page six says about us."

"But you're *not* genuine, you do what gets you views. Staged entertainment."

Tristan's words hit a nerve. How dare he. It's bad enough the public judges me, but to have Tristan imply that I'm vapid and fake cuts deeper than the negative comments I get from strangers.

Slamming the remote down, I stand and leave.

I went up to my room and slept for a few hours. With nothing to do, my body has no energy to even stay awake. I'm not used to this much free time, and I don't like it.

Hearty smells fill the house and I know Tristan is cooking something, so I decide to get out of bed.

"Are you hungry?" Tristan asks as soon as I walk downstairs.

"A little."

"Take a seat, I'll bring you some spaghetti."

I'm surprised he's even talking to me, but considering my parents pay him, he doesn't have a choice.

"Would you like parmesan?"

"Sure, thanks." I pull out a chair and sit, in the mood for some comfort carbs.

The sun is setting, reflecting a gorgeous hue over the water, and I wish I could go out there and relax.

"Garlic bread?"

"Just one."

Moments later, Tristan brings over a plateful. "Thank you."

"Hope it's edible and to your liking."

There's his condescending attitude.

"It's pretty hard to screw up spaghetti but I guess if anyone could, it'd be you," I sing-song.

"You know how to cook?" he challenges, arching a brow as he walks back to the kitchen.

"I can manage the basics," I reply.

He returns to the table with his own plate and sits across from me. "Like what? Maybe I'll add the ingredients to the list so you can pull your weight around here."

"Are we a domestic couple now? We're taking turns cooking for one another?" I muse, twirling my fork in the noodles.

"We could be here for a while and you've already said I'm a bad cook so having you make something might be better."

27

"I never said that, I just had a *couple* of suggestions," I correct, then take a bite. "And this isn't terrible."

"So glad to hear you approve," he says dryly.

"Fine, I'll make grilled cheese with tomatoes, but I need Sourdough bread."

"How do you manage to make a simple recipe into something bougie?"

I bark out a laugh. "That's not bougie! Sourdough bread is healthier than white bread and it tastes better. It's a personal preference." I shrug.

"That's because you've never struggled or had limited options. If you had, you'd have learned to appreciate whatever you had, even if it were moldy bread and expired cheese."

"What makes you think I don't appreciate things just because I have money to buy what I like? That seems judgy."

"Well first, I've worked for your family for the past six months, and have watched you very closely. I see what you do and how you act, and have drawn my own conclusions. It's not unreasonable to think that your privilege is why you are the way you are. You've never had a bad day in your life."

I grind my teeth, growing angry by his unfair assessment. "Wow. Glad to know what you really think of me when you've taken all of two seconds to get to know me. Meanwhile, you hide in the shadows, glaring at life as if you were purposely dealt a bad hand. You've watched me and kept to yourself, dedicating your life to someone else's instead of living your own. So tell me what that really says about you?"

"I fought for our country and now devote my life to protecting others. Doesn't mean I haven't lived. I'm certain I've seen more in my thirty-seven years than you'll see in a lifetime."

"Sorry I'm not a thirty-seven-year-old man with a stick up my ass. If I were, maybe then you'd see me as something more than an heirloom princess who's *never had a bad day in her life*," I mock his words, then stand and walk away.

The past two days are the most Tristan and I have ever spoken to one another and maybe it's best if we don't talk. He only sees the superficial parts of my life, but it's like he doesn't care to learn more. He's already decided what kind of person I am.

An hour passes before I hear footsteps and Tristan enters without knocking.

"You stormed off before I could give you this." He holds out a phone and I sit up. "It's a burner phone, nothing special. You won't be able to download apps or access the internet, but you can call or text your family."

My shoulders slump, but at least I can speak to my sister, so I take it. "Thanks."

"You can go outside on the small patio that's fenced in, but that's it. I'll be making sure you don't go outside of the perimeter."

"Jesus, you act like I'm a murderer or something."

"Unless you want to *get* murdered, you'll do as I say," he retorts before leaving.

I roll my eyes when he's no longer in view, then turn on the phone. It's already programmed with Kendall's and my parents' cell phone numbers.

If these restrictions don't make me feel like a damn child, I don't know what will.

Instead of pouting, I head outside to chat with Kendall since I know she's the most worried about me.

"Pipes?"

"Yeah, it's me. Am I interrupting wedding sex?" I ask, leaning back on a chair.

"Don't worry, we've already banged three times since last night. Ryan's probably grateful for the break." She snickers.

"Geez, you trying to get knocked up already or what?"

"Obviously, my eggs aren't getting any younger. But enough about me, where are you?"

"Florida, on a beach, but I don't know where exactly. My prison guard won't let me lay out. I'm lucky he even let me outside."

"I thought you were excited to be trapped with your sexy bodyguard? Pretty sure those were your exact words."

"I was until he turned into ice. He's much hotter when he's not talking."

"Piper!" She scolds. "You need to be nice and understanding. He probably doesn't want to be there either and is risking his life for you. Give him a chance."

"He thinks I'm a spoiled little princess," I say with a groan.

"You are," Ryan says in the background.

"I heard that!" I shout, looking up at the evening sky.

Sighing, I continue. "It's one thing for strangers and the media to make ridiculous claims, but I thought he'd have a higher opinion since he's around me so often."

"How much does he really know you, though? He's followed you around from event to event, fancy dinners, and elite parties. This is your chance to really show him that there's more to you than what meets the eye. Don't be a brat, and he won't think you are one."

I grunt, but she has a point. Tristan knows Piper, the socialite. He's never seen me relax and enjoy life outside of the camera.

"Guess you're right," I admit.

"I usually am," she gloats.

"Yeah, yeah, yeah. He's also sixteen years older than me, like a whole different generation. He probably grew up with dial-up internet."

Ryan chuckles. "Most millennials did."

"Try to take this time to reset and let the police do their job. They'll find this guy soon enough, and then you'll be back to your limelight reality."

"So I guess this would be a bad time to tell you there's no air-conditioning, the food sucks, and my bed is as comfortable as a dog crate?"

"And I thought you were the dramatic one," Ryan murmurs.

"Tell your *husband* to shut his mouth. I bet you were the same way last year when you were without electricity and water," I say smugly. There's no way in hell Kendall didn't complain about their living conditions when they were snowed-in.

"Hell yes, she was," Ryan confirms. "And she was as every bit dramatic and whiny as you sound."

"I would've thought getting laid six ways to Sunday would make Ryan a little more likable. Guess not," I deadpan.

"He's just teasing you, Pipe. He picks on me for all my high-maintenance shit too. That's how he shows love," Kendall reassures, but I'm not buying it.

Ryan's an ER doctor who works long hours in a New York City hospital. He went to med school and devoted his life to helping people, so I find it hard to stay mad at him even when he teases me. His sister Cami is just as spoiled as us.

I snort. "I'd hate to see how he acts toward someone he dislikes."

31

"He acts like you don't even exist. Trust me, that's worse than his teasing," Kendall says, knowing from experience.

"So with that knowledge, the moment Tristan starts ignoring me completely, I've lost my chance."

"Yep. Guys won't put in any sort of effort if they're not interested," Kendall confirms. "Just be yourself, and he'll warm up to you in no time."

I scoff. *Doubtful*. Very doubtful.

CHAPTER FOUR

TRISTAN

DAY 2

PIPER HAS WALKED around the house like she's the star of a zombie movie when the camera isn't in her face. I find it entertaining, even if she's ready to kill me.

I grab an apple off the kitchen counter and bite into it. She's sitting on the couch and turns her head. Her eyes trail up and down my body before she meets my gaze again.

"Will you be wearing guns the entire time we're here?"

I take another bite, crunching down. "The only time they won't be on me is when I'm sleeping or bathing. Otherwise, they'll *always* be locked and loaded."

"Don't you think you're overreacting just a little bit?"

"No. I have to always be ready."

She turns back around. "Guns make me uncomfortable. There are a ton of statistics out there that prove having them puts you in more danger than not."

I laugh. "Absolutely. Those stats are for those who don't have the experience I have. I've been heavily trained for combat and war. I'm not your average Joe. If someone tries to disarm me and use my weapons against me, good luck. They'll need it."

"Cocky much?" She flicks through the channels as I sit at the bar and finish my fruit.

After fifteen minutes of her not finding anything to watch, I clear my throat. "Why don't we play a game or do a puzzle?"

She gives me a death glare.

I meet her eyes. "Have you ever done either?"

She scoffs but doesn't answer. It's obvious she hasn't, and it makes me more curious about her childhood. I wonder what it was like to be a Montgomery. They're one of the richest families in the world, billionaires who come from old oil money. Maybe one day I'll ask, but for now, I'll assume it was full of afternoon tea and croquet.

I go to the closet under the stairs where we keep everything. Several boxes of puzzles have been collecting dust for years, maybe decades. My mother used to buy them for the beach house every chance she got, so many haven't been opened.

I place several on the table, giving her a few choices. Piper comes and stands beside me, intrigued.

"You can pick."

I think I see a small smile on her lips, but she pushes it back. "What about this one?"

She points at the five-thousand-piece sailboat one.

"It's rated at level four, which means difficult."

She shrugs. "I like the picture."

"Alright, let's do it." I open and dump the box on the large dining room table. Piper watches as I flip the pieces upright. She leans over and helps me.

I lean the box upright, so we have some sort of key.

"I like to put the border together first, then work my way to the middle," I explain.

She nods and begins putting all the ones that have flat edges to the side. Soon she's snapped a few together, and I realize it's the top, so I scoot them in place.

I reach forward and attach one to it, and then she follows with another. Each time they lock together, she smiles wider.

"Do you do this a lot?" she asks, meeting my eyes.

"Not much anymore. We'd always have a puzzle on the dining room table when I was growing up. Each time we'd walk by, we'd work on it until it was finally complete. Once we'd get close to the end, we'd race each other to finish just for the satisfaction of putting the final piece in place."

She laughs. "Really?"

"Yeah, sometimes it would take weeks. Mom started mod podging and framing them until we eventually ran out of wall space."

Piper laughs. "I noticed the beach one hanging in my room."

"Yeah, It was good times." I grin, remembering when we finished it.

"Sounds like it." Piper grabs her camera, only this time I'm not sure if she's acting or being genuine when she presses record.

"Guys! Look what I'm doing right now!" she says directly into the lens, then turns it around to show them. I find it kind of adorable she's this excited about something so simple. She films herself finding a few that fit together then zooms in on the box. "I can't wait to show you the finished product!"

I'm not sure I'll ever get used to her vlogging, but I've mastered staying out of her way.

After a few more minutes, she grows bored and eventually

returns to the living room. My phone rings, and I step outside. Considering a wall of windows faces the beach, I still keep my eyes on Piper.

"Hey, Mom," I say with a grin when I answer.

"Tristan! How was the flight? How's the beach house? Are you coming to visit us?"

"Whoa, that's a lot of questions at once." I blow out a breath. "Everything's fine, but no, I won't be able to see you guys right now. I'm on special business and can't leave."

"Oh," she says, and I can hear the disappointment in her tone. "We miss you, son."

"I miss you and Dad too. I promise I'll make it up to you once everything settles down on my end."

"Are you in danger?" she blurts out.

I feel bad for lying, but I don't want her to worry. "Not really. Nothing I can't handle. Just a stalker situation."

"Tristan!"

"Mom, please don't start. You promised you wouldn't when I decided to take this job, remember?"

She sighs. "I know, it's just hard after everything. I want you to stay safe."

"I'm safe now that I'm at the beach house. Appreciate you letting us use it."

"Do you know how long you'll be there?"

I glance out at the waves and the white sand. "Not yet. Could be a few days, could be weeks. Only time will tell."

"If things change, come see us. Oh, and your dad sends his love."

"I will. Love you and Dad both. I'll keep in touch."

"Let me know if you need anything, okay? We'll be happy to take a drive and bring whatever you need."

"Thanks, Mom. Love you."

"I love you too."

I end the call and go inside where Piper is laid back on the couch with her feet propped up.

"I think I'm going to take a shower. I'm sticky and hot," she announces when I walk into the kitchen.

"Alright."

She gets up and goes upstairs like she hates life. I chuckle, wondering if Piper was an unbearable teenager who hated following her parents' rules.

The TV blares, and before I turn it off, I realize she was watching an internet entertainment show, and they're discussing all the drama in the beauty community. It's so much, I can't even keep up with who's the villain in this situation. They all seem insane. I hear the water turn on upstairs, then go to the table and add more pieces to the puzzle in silence.

Eventually, my phone buzzes in my pocket, and I pull it out.

Easton: Doing okay?

Tristan: Of course.

His text bubble immediately pops up.

Easton: How's everything going? The princess surviving?

Tristan: As best she can.

Easton: So, when were you gonna tell me you're working for someone as famous as her? Have you

googled her? She's literally like the JoJo Siwa of our time.

I shake my head.

Tristan: I'm aware of the details of my client.

Easton: Oh, talking to me like you're all business.

He inserts an eye roll emoji.

Easton: Dude, she has millions of followers. There are pictures of her on Instagram with megastars. This is blowing my damn mind.

Tristan: Well, if she's so popular, how come you didn't know who she was when you saw her?

Easton: Because I only just realized. Plus, I'm too busy surfing to stay up-to-date with pop culture.

Before working for the Montgomery's, I had no idea what the big deal was when it came to Piper. After the first month, I asked myself several times if I had lived in a damn cave because it seemed like everyone knew who she was. She's been asked to present Grammys and Kid's Choice Awards. There have been a few blockbuster hit movies where she had cameos too. Piper's done so much at such a young age, and I find it impressive, regardless if I had no clue who she was. Granted, I liked to spend my free time outdoors rather than glued behind a computer screen, but to each their own.

I try to change the subject, not wanting to discuss her any longer.

Tristan: So when will you be able to stop by?

Easton: This Friday. I work a half-day and was planning to go surfing afterward, but instead, I'm acting as your personal assistant. Haha, don't let this celebrity shit get to your head.

Tristan: Very funny. And that sounds good. I'll see you then.

Piper eventually returns, and her wet hair is thrown up into a bun. She doesn't give me a second glance as she walks to her phone and picks it up. Disappointment covers her face when she sees no one has called or texted. She groans, grabs her camera, then goes to the back door. Before she steps outside, I stop her.

"I'd prefer you didn't."

She gives me a death glare. "Do you think the boogeyman is going to get me in broad daylight while you're packing two guns on your chest?"

I glare at her. "You have no idea who will recognize you."

"Didn't you say this was a *private* beach?"

I nod. "Yes, but that just means private access. Anyone could be out there, and you know how recognizable you are, even from a distance. There's really no safe place for you other than inside the house and the fenced-in patio area."

She clenches her jaw. "This is total shit. I need vitamin D. By the time I come out of hiding, I'm gonna look like Casper the freaking ghost in the middle of summer instead of being my usual sun-kissed self."

I hold back laughter because I'm not trying to poke the beast. So I don't say anything and just continue with the puzzle. Instead of arguing, she sits across from me and taps her fingers on the wood. I've become a pro at tuning her out, even when she's staring at me so intensely.

She eventually gives up and goes back to the living room where she melts into the couch. If I didn't know better, I'd say she was wishing it would swallow her whole. Unfortunately, there's nothing I can do but let her frustration run its course. I wasn't hired to be her entertainment.

"I just don't understand why we couldn't have gone to my parents' mountain cabin or to their London penthouse or even the Hawaiian villa. Why are we *here*?"

I contemplate ignoring her. "You're smarter than that, Piper."

"What do you mean? At least we'd have plenty of amenities—a home gym, indoor heated pool, and air-conditioning. This is the bottom of the barrel."

"You don't think Jack has the addresses to every place your parents own? Or that the paps won't be waiting for you to show up at one of them? Think about it. The only reason you're safe here and won't be found is because this place isn't on anyone's radar."

She clenches her jaw, knowing I'm right.

"That doesn't make this any less painful," she mumbles.

"Yeah, well, it's not my idea of fun either."

She acts offended, grabs her camera, and then marches upstairs. I wait for a door to slam, but surprisingly, it doesn't happen.

CHAPTER FIVE

PIPER

DAY 4

I FEEL like I'm losing my mind. It's gotten to a point where
time seems to be standing completely still, and I'm just going
through the motions until another boring day approaches.
Though I can call and text on the burner phone, there isn't
much else I can do on it. I'm trying not to bother my sister
since she's on her honeymoon. My parents have zero
sympathy for my lack of necessities and remind me it's only
temporary.

I swear, I will never take the small things for granted again.
Grocery delivery, laying out, air-conditioning, and my
freedom to do whatever I want whenever I want. The
humidity in Florida near the coast is deadly, and I hate it. Not
to mention, the beach house looks like it was last updated in
the sixties.

My smooth and silky hair hasn't made an appearance since
I've not had my stay-in conditioner. Now it's a frizzy,
unmanageable mess, and I've tried to come to terms with it. If

I'd known that this excursion would last more than a couple of days, I'd have brought an extra suitcase. I'm pissed at myself for not being prepared and having to depend on other people to get what I need. I've never been in a situation like this before, and it better be the last time.

Easton still hasn't come with the things I put on my list, and I'm growing annoyed that I don't know when he's coming. With Tristan around twenty-four seven, he's more like my boss than my shadow, and it's something I'm trying to get used to. I'm not one to take orders from anyone, but he's not the type who'll let me have my way. Sure, I've tried to skirt the lines a few times, but he wasn't allowing it.

I wish I could log in to my social media for just five minutes, check my accounts, post, and then ghost. At least I could explain my absence then. This makes it feel like I'm detoxing, and unfortunately, this place is much worse than rehab. At least when my friends went, they were served gourmet meals, had hot tubs, daily massages, and were treated like pure royalty. Meanwhile, I feel like I'm at one of Dr. Phil's retreats for troubled youth.

I lie in bed and realize I can't stay here all day, so I grab my backpack with my gear and go downstairs. I need to get some work done and catch up on editing.

When I make it to the bottom of the stairs, Tristan's sitting at the breakfast bar drinking a cup of coffee and reading a book.

"Afternoon."

"You too," I say, knowing I've been awake since eight and just refused to come downstairs. I check the time on the microwave, and it says it's 12:42 p.m. My stomach grumbles, so I set my bag down and open the fridge. Nothing looks appetizing, so I shut it.

"When's Easton coming?"

"My brother's busy running his shop. Summer is one of his busiest seasons, so he'll get here when he gets here."

I shake my head, not appreciating the snark in his tone. I've never had someone be so brash toward me. Most try to get on my good side, but Tristan gives no fucks. I guess this is what it's like to be treated like everyone else.

Once I grab a banana from the counter, I pour myself a cup of coffee. Since we have no creamer, I drink it black but hate how it tastes. Desperate times call for desperate measures, though, so I suck it up.

Deciding to set up my workspace for the day, I sit at the long table on the opposite end of the puzzle.

As soon as I open my laptop and pull out memory cards, Tristan meets my eyes.

"I know. No internet. You've already reminded me a million times."

He wears a flat expression. "You're right."

"Don't you realize I have a VPN installed? Do you even know what that is?" I'd be willing to bet he doesn't.

"Do you?" he retorts.

"Of course, it stands for…" I hesitate, trying to remember.

"Virtual Private Network," he states before I can think of it. "I'm well aware of what it does and how you can change your IP address and location *once* it's connected."

"Okay, smart-ass."

He lifts a brow. "We've both learned recently that Jack is smarter than the average stalker. If he hacked your phone, then I'm convinced that laptop has the same tracker on it. Without shipping it to the authorities, like your father suggested, there's no way to know what's infiltrating it."

My eyes go wide. "My dad wanted to send it somewhere?"

"Yes, but I suggested he wait until Jack's caught, so then you could at least get some work done while you're here. I know your whole life is on that thing and how devastating it would've been without it."

I meet his eyes. "Not sure how you pulled that off."

"He's not an easy man to convince, but I gave him my word that you wouldn't have online access, so he agreed."

"Wow, thanks," I tell him, putting my memory card in and dragging over the gigs of video I took before the wedding.

"You're welcome. When I give someone my word, I don't break that promise. So don't make me out to be a liar to your father."

"I won't," I say, regardless of how much I wish I could. If I did, my father would show up with an entourage of men to take my laptop and bring me somewhere else. Tristan's bad attitude is at least growing on me. I'd much rather deal with him than ten men who won't look me in the eye and pretend I'm invisible.

After I've transferred over twenty hours of footage, I open my editing software and add clips to my timeline. It's almost hard for me to watch these videos, seeing how happy and careless I was. I love vlogging and always have my camera with me everywhere I go. Between that and my phone, I can capture nearly my entire day. While I don't show every little detail, I give my viewers enough to make them want more.

"Shit," I say, opening my planner and realizing I need to post a sponsored video on Thursday.

"What?" Tristan asks.

I shake my head. "I didn't schedule my sponsored posts. *Fuck*." I place my face in my hands, trying not to get upset. I'm pissed at myself for procrastinating instead of getting ahead like I promised I would. It was hard to stay on schedule with pre-wedding celebrations and everything else, but I've never missed posting, especially when I'm being paid.

"It'll be okay."

"No, it won't. You don't understand." I groan.

"Maybe I do?"

I shake my head, with emotions ready to bubble over. "That video was supposed to go up tomorrow for this designer perfume company. Now, it'll seem like I didn't follow through and will be put in the same bucket as those content creators who use and abuse brands."

"Piper…" Tristan says in a growl of a tone that has goose bumps trailing over my body. "You could've died the night of your sister's wedding. You realize that, don't you?"

I meet his eyes.

"If Jack would've had a weapon or somehow managed to drag you away, you might not be here right now. In the grand scheme of things, do you really think that perfume is *that* important?" His words linger for a few moments.

"Compared to my life? No."

"So just explain what happened when things calm down. I'm sure they'll understand that you were in a very dangerous and vulnerable situation."

"And what if they don't?" A few tears roll down my cheeks.

"Then fuck 'em. I'm sure they need you more than you need them anyway. You don't want to work with selfish companies who don't care about your well-being."

My face cracks into a smile, and I laugh, something I needed more than he'll ever know.

"You want me to make you a sandwich?" he asks, noticing the banana I haven't touched.

"Not really."

He closes his book and goes to the pantry. His guns are attached to his body, just as he promised they would be. "You have to eat something."

Tristan opens the pantry and pulls out a box of mac 'n' cheese. Once he's done cooking, he sets a bowl in front of me with a fork and napkin.

"This is *a lot* of cheese."

He shrugs. "You're the one who said you still eat dairy."

Tristan adds a few pieces to the puzzle before going to the couch. As soon as he's out of sight, I take a bite, and it's so damn delicious, I have another. Soon, the bowl is empty, and I'm tempted to lick the cheese sauce from the bottom but refrain.

When I'm done, I busy myself with my work and start cutting and placing clips together so they'll flow better. After I've gotten one of my days down to a good length, I open my commercial music folder and find something that fits the different moods.

I love planning my days before they happen and having an underlying story and theme. In this vlog, I went shopping for new face wash and summer sandals. Halfway through, I realized I didn't have my credit card, but luckily, I was able to use Apple Pay. It was a clever way to sneak in a sponsored shoutout since they send me all the new electronics before they release to the public. It comes off dramatic in the video, but it's because I set up the scene. My audience loves it when things like this happen, and I get so much joy when I read the comments. Most of them are cheering me on.

As I continue scanning through the footage at the mall, I think I see a familiar face in the background.

"Oh my God," I gasp, covering a hand over my mouth.

Tristan stands and comes over as I study the video.

"Is that Jack in the food court watching me?"

"Fuck, I think it *is* him," he confirms, and I go into a panic.

I look up at Tristan. "He's been following me around since last week then."

"What day was this recorded?" Tristan asks as I find the timestamp. "It was Thursday around one."

"*Bastard*," he mutters. "Do you have other videos from that day?"

Tristan pulls a chair beside me, and we go through every frame of when I'm in public.

"Right there," he says, and I press the spacebar to stop it. "Can you zoom in?"

I make the window bigger.

"I think that's him on the street wearing a hat. Go forward some," he tells me.

In the footage I'm taking, I walk right past Jack, holding the camera up as I speak into it. I now see an evil grin on Jack's face as his beady eyes stare me down. A shiver runs up my spine, knowing how close he was to me on several different occasions.

No telling what could've happened if Tristan hadn't been with me. While it's annoying that he's always around, and sometimes I feel awkward filming in front of him, I'm glad he was there. Tristan was on high alert because I decided to vlog in public to mix up my content. At first, he was against it but agreed after my father approved. I'd already filmed a lot of things in my apartment and needed a different setting.

I glance over at Tristan, and his nostrils flare.

"I had no idea he was in New York," I whisper, staring at the deranged man on the screen.

"He was too chickenshit to try anything. It's almost like he was hoping for attention at your sister's wedding. Like he's trying to get a headline or something."

"I thought about that, actually."

"So did your dad. It's why he's paid the newspapers and magazines not to run the stories because word that someone broke into the event has spread."

"Damn," I whisper-hiss, the guilt of what happened still sits on my shoulders.

Tristan notices my demeanor change. "It's not your fault, Piper."

I shrug with a frown. "Doesn't make me feel any better."

We finish scanning through more footage and don't see Jack in any more frames. Tristan excuses himself to call my father and tell him what we found.

An eerie feeling creeps over me that this man has been following me in broad daylight, and I had no idea.

I decide to close my laptop and take a break. Though I'm halfway done editing the video, I'm not even sure I'll post it now.

Infiltrating my life has probably been his intention all along, and I hope to God they find him sooner than later.

CHAPTER SIX

TRISTAN

DAY 6

IT'S BEEN a couple of days since we found out Jack was in New York following Piper. Mr. Montgomery was pissed when I told him, but he wasn't shocked, considering the photos and threats he sent. Since he hacked Piper's cell phone, it's not out of the realm of possibilities that Jack knew exactly where she was at all times. I'm almost positive he was waiting to get her alone so he could follow through with his plan. Unfortunately for him, I was always next to her, and I'm sure that frustrated him.

Could be why he crashed the wedding.

Anytime Piper was out of the house, I didn't let her out of my sight and was usually within arm's length. The paparazzi made comments and asked if I was her boyfriend, but Piper never confirmed or denied it. She's twenty-one and is just starting her adult life. Meanwhile, I've been through hell and back.

I'm sure when we return to New York, we won't talk as

much, and the invisible wall will be put up again. It's fine with me. Piper has tried her hardest to get me to open up before now, but I've refused to allow myself to do that.

The Montgomerys are *very* protective of their daughter and pay me extremely well to keep her safe at all costs. I've vowed to protect her like she's the fucking president and will take a bullet for her too.

After I'm dressed and go downstairs, I find Piper recording as she sits in front of the windows that face the ocean. She's upbeat as she talks about what she's been doing. I quietly move into the kitchen, then lean against the counter and watch her.

"And it's been such a relaxing vacation, guys. I can't tell you how amazing it's been given the circumstances, but I'd highly recommend you all take a moment to yourself every once in a while. Enjoy the sunshine and work on your mental health. Anyway, love you guys." She blows a kiss toward the camera and then waves, like usual, before ending the video.

I lift a brow at her and smirk.

"What?" She scowls

"Nothing." I shake my head, then fill the coffee pot with water and add some grounds.

"It's obvious you have something you wanted to say."

"Just wondering why you're so different when the camera is on compared to how you are in real life?"

She rolls her eyes. "We've talked about this, Tristan. It's social media. You get to be whoever you want online. On YouTube, I'm Miss Positivity, who can always find the bright side of every situation."

"So, you're playing a character? Like an actress."

"No, I wouldn't go that far. I really do try to find the silver linings about life. I'm me. It's just my online personality is an extreme version of me. There's enough negativity in the world today, so if I can be a slice of sunshine with an overly bubbly personality, then I will."

"Hmm," I say, pulling a mug from the cabinet.

"What's so wrong with that?"

"I just think you're doing your audience a disservice. Your true authentic self is more enjoyable and relatable. Instead of being this mega-wealthy and famous YouTuber whose biggest problem in life is running out of your favorite eye shadow, you should show them who you really are."

"And who is that exactly?"

"A twentysomething woman who has real-life issues outside of the glitz and glam. More than what the media shows. You don't share that, and honestly, I don't know anyone who can relate to a person who has a perfect life. But then again, it's just my opinion. What do I know?"

"Well, apparently, I'm doing something right, considering my subscriber count and how many Instagram followers I have. They like what I have to say and share."

"Sure. But eventually, the act will drop. You can't pretend to be someone you're not forever."

We stare each other down for a few seconds, but I don't push it any further. There are two different Pipers, and it depends on if the camera is rolling and people are watching or if she's let her guard down and relaxing. I can't imagine trying to be someone I'm not all the time. It has to be exhausting, but I keep that thought to myself.

After eating breakfast and drinking my coffee, I hear a loud booming knock on the door. Piper jumps and looks over at me. I walk over with a hand on my gun. Quickly, I check the peephole, then realize it's Easton.

I swing the door open and scowl. "Why the fuck did you knock like you're the goddamn police?"

Easton chuckles. "Wanted to make sure you heard me."

His hands are full, and I notice his trunk is still open.

"I'll grab the rest," I tell him as he heads inside.

I carry as much as I can, but it's going to take another trip. Considering Piper gave him a hell of a list, I'm not surprised there are so many.

After the car's unloaded, Piper opens a few bags and digs out some items.

"What's all of this?" she asks.

"It's some of the things you asked for," he tells her.

"Recipe books, crossword puzzles, adult coloring books, and pencils." Her eyes go wide with confusion. "I'm not five."

I clear my throat. "You were bored and needed some stuff to do. I told Easton to use his imagination."

"This is a joke, right?" She's holding a box of ultra absorption tampons.

Easton chuckles as Piper's face turns beet red.

"Just in case Mother Nature was as *extra* as you," he explains with a shit-eating smirk.

Piper chews on the inside of her mouth like she's ready to curse Easton a mouthful. She continues to pull things out with disdain. "I asked for a *bikini*."

"And that's a one-piece bathing suit," Easton says.

She shakes her head. "This will give me tan lines galore."

"You won't be going outside to worry about that. Plus, the last time I checked, there's no one here for you to impress," I state.

"You're absolutely right about that since *neither* of you is my type." She looks between Easton and me.

Since I've been around, Piper hasn't dated anyone, so I'm

not sure what her type is. She's married to her job, and while her sister and friends have tried to set her up, she's always blown them off. She could get *anyone* she wants—man or woman—without even trying, but she hasn't seemed interested.

Piper unloads more items. "Oh, thank God. Fresh veggies and fruit." She glances at Easton. "Okay, I officially forgive you for all the other bullshit."

He places his hand over his heart. "Thank you. Now I'll be able to sleep tonight knowing that Piper Montgomery has graciously forgiven me for my sins."

She rolls her eyes. "So does being a smart-ass run in the family?"

"Yes," Easton and I say at the same time, then burst into laughter.

"You're worse than me, though," he says.

"Yeah, right. Mom told me how much of a dick you are to work for," I throw back.

"Whatever, my employees have the best boss. Handsome, charming, and I pay well."

"Screams arrogant," Piper adds with a smirk.

"Yeah, well, I didn't have the military to straighten me up like Tristan. I'd rather be arrogant than a hard-ass."

I groan, not wanting to talk about my past. "I'm not."

"Yes, you're actually all of the above. I get the best of both worlds, I guess," she muses with a forced smile.

Easton chuckles as he helps Piper put away the food. "Doesn't matter how many months go by without seeing him, his arrogance and stuck-up attitude never changes," he tells her.

"I think you mean more mature and wiser. Don't worry, brother, that comes with age." I grin at him, knowing how much he hates it when I joke about how much younger he is than me.

"Wait, you don't see each other that much?" Piper asks.

"Not really," I admit.

She turns to me. "How long has it been?"

"A year? Maybe two?"

Easton nods. "Yeah, that sounds about right."

"Oh my God. I'd kill someone if I didn't get to see my sister as much as I wanted. You should stay for dinner," she suggests.

"That's a good idea. I was going to make Hawaiian chicken and veggies," I say, and we continue filling the pantry and fridge with groceries.

He grins. "I don't have much else going on. I went surfing early this morning."

"Great!" Piper squeals. "Then you can answer all the questions Tristan has straight-up ignored since we met."

Easton chuckles. "I dunno. Tristan's pretty scary and might kick my ass."

I shake my head. "How about we not talk about my past or me at all?"

Easton's expression softens. He knows everything, but it has been brought up since it all happened. There's too much to explain to someone like Piper, and the thoughts that come from talking about it are better buried away.

"How about you tell me about yourself, Piper. Apparently, you're a big deal or something," my brother says. Once everything has been put away, we move to the living room to finish the conversation. Piper and I sit at opposite ends while Easton plops down in the middle.

"I'm not," she humbly replies, but every person in this room knows that's a lie, even her.

Easton snorts. "Okay. Since you're not a big deal, maybe you can pimp my surf shop when you're released from this… what did you call it? *Prison*?"

Piper grins. "Might cost ya."

"Exactly. That's what I thought." He laughs.

When she pops a brow, I immediately know that she's up to no good.

"Just answer a few questions, and it'll be a deal." She holds out her hand, and Easton looks at me before shaking it.

"Sorry, bro. There's no way I could ever afford a shout-out from *the* Piper Montgomery."

"What a sell-out!" I grunt.

He shrugs unapologetically. "Free marketing. Gotta take business opportunities when I can."

"There's no such thing as a free lunch. It's the basic principles of economics," I remind him.

"Yeah, yeah, save it," Piper says, then turns to Easton. "You gotta tell me how Tristan was growing up."

"Just the way that he is right now, but not as buff. Same dry personality."

She chuckles. "Why am I not surprised?"

"He's eleven years older than me, so…"

"Wait, how old are you?" Piper asks him.

"Twenty-six, about to be twenty-seven."

"And you already started your own business?"

He nods proudly. "Yep. Opened it two years ago."

"And you brought me a grandma bathing suit?" She gives him an evil eye.

"I take it you don't surf." He snickers.

She sarcastically laughs. "No. I barely swim, though I did take lessons when I was younger because my mother was paranoid. I wasn't the strongest kid out there, though."

"That grandma bathing suit is one of the most expensive brands we carry—Shan. It isn't cheap, and athletes wear them," he informs her.

"It has sleeves, Easton. Sleeves! I'd be better off wearing my bra and panties outside."

"Wouldn't happen," I bark out, deciding to get up and start dinner. It's just past five, and I'm actually hungry. As I chop the pineapple and jalapeño into pico-sized chunks, Piper and Easton move to the breakfast bar and continue chatting.

"What kind of women does Tristan like?"

Easton hesitates. "You know, I'm not sure anymore. When I was younger, I remember he dated a girl from England. Foreign exchange student. But I was only seven when he graduated high school and left for boot camp."

"Wow, so you didn't really get to grow up together for long. English student, huh? How'd you pull that off?" Piper asks me.

"I'm not talking about my past relationships with you," I state, quickly shutting her down before she gets any more ideas.

"You're really no fun."

"I wasn't hired to be." I sear the chicken breasts in the skillet as I put some black beans in a pot. Then I sauté some broccoli.

"So what about you?" Easton asks her, and I'm actually interested in her answer. I glance over my shoulder as she hesitates, biting on her bottom lip.

"I haven't dated much, honestly. Most guys my age are immature and only want to use me for who I am or the attention my name can give them. Not to mention, my parents have impossibly high standards for who I should marry, which makes it hard to date. Right now, I'm happily single and not really looking. I stay plenty busy without a man tying me down. But of course, that could all change if the right person came into my life. I have an open mind."

"Me too. I'm not actively dating, but if someone special comes into my life, that could change," Easton admits.

If my brother is flirting with Piper, I swear to God, I might lose my shit.

"I mean, not with the parent thing. My mom and dad have loved everyone I've brought home. It's just hard to find someone my age whose personality isn't all about bar hopping and drinking. I don't go out much, so most girls in their twenties can't relate. I take my business really seriously. I love the ocean and being outside. Just can't seem to find a woman who likes the same."

"Wow, yes. I understand that more than you know. Partying is fun once in a while, but after once or twice, I'm over it. I'd rather hang out and spend quality time with someone," she says, and then they sit in silence.

By the time I was twenty-five, I had felt like I'd already lived a lifetime and had traveled all over the world. So, I really can't relate to either of them. I'm sixteen years older than Piper and was practically an adult when she was born. After graduation, I signed my life over to the military, hoping after serving for twenty years, I'd retire and settle down. Except that didn't quite work out the way I planned.

As the conversation comes to a lull, I interrupt them. "Dinner is almost ready."

I pull out plates from the cabinet, and they come over. The whole house smells amazing, and I can't wait to dig into my food.

Once we sit at the open end of the table, Easton finally spots the puzzle. "No way."

It puts a smile on my face. "It's been a while, hasn't it?"

"Yeah. It really has."

Easton scoots a little closer to the pieces and starts placing them together, building on what Piper and I have already completed.

"Hey! Don't do too much. That thing has to last me God knows how long," she scolds, and he chuckles.

"I could literally sit here all night and work on it." He turns the box around to view the picture.

"Shoulda told me to pick one up. There's a souvenir shop a few blocks away that sells the really hard ones."

"Next time," Piper says, taking a big bite of chicken.

I meet her big blue eyes. "Wait, you like doing puzzles now?"

"I don't mind it. Might have to take my new hobby back to New York with me. What's the biggest one you've done?"

I have to think about it. "Might've been seventy-five hundred pieces. The largest puzzle you can buy is fifty-thousand pieces, I think."

Piper's eyes widen. "Seriously? I can't imagine how long that'd take to put together. Where could you even put something that big?"

"Months. Hell, maybe years," Easton says, then adds. "You'd need a big penthouse or something…"

"Ha! Consider yourself officially invited to come build a fifty-thousand-piece puzzle with me. Even you, Tristan."

I scoff. "Thanks."

Piper takes a few more bites as if she hasn't eaten all day and releases a throaty moan that echoes through the room. "This is so delicious."

"Glad you approve this time," I say, trying to ignore how my body reacts to her.

After we've finished our dinner, Easton offers to clean the kitchen. Piper tells us she's going to take a shower, and I sit at the breakfast bar.

"Thanks for staying for dinner. It was good to see you for more than a few minutes," I say.

"No problem. Glad I could. Don't get to see you nearly enough."

"I know. Might need to change that as soon as things settle down," I admit.

"I'd like that. Maybe go and catch some waves."

A small smile hits my lips. "You know, I haven't done that in over a decade."

I think back to the last time I was on a board. It was before I left for basic training. Things were much different back then, though. I was more carefree and less jaded.

"You just tell me when, and I'll clear my schedule," he tells me, wiping the plates dry before placing them in the cabinet. "Piper isn't as snobby as I imagined she'd be."

I smile. "She's humble and down to earth. Only snarky when she's miserable."

"Bet this is actually pretty hard for her."

"Yeah, but I think she's finally adjusting. It's only temporary, and soon, she'll be back in her New York penthouse." I shrug.

"Do you know how much longer you guys have to stay here?"

I shake my head. "No idea. Playing it all by ear right now."

He dries his hands and faces me. "Well, I'll bring you shit for as long as you need. Don't hesitate to call or text me, okay?"

"Sure. Thanks again for helping out."

"Yeah, anytime. Guess I should probably go before the traffic gets too crazy."

I stand and give him a hug. "We should do this again."

He pulls away and smirks. "We absolutely should. Tell Piper I said thanks for a good time."

"Yeah, yeah."

Easton heads toward the door, and I follow him, then wave as he backs out of the driveway.

After I lock up, I sit on the couch and turn on the TV. Twenty minutes later, Piper comes back downstairs with her hair wrapped in a towel and plops down next to me.

"Your brother is nice."

"He can be."

"He seems to bring out the good side in you."

I glance over at her. "He does. He's my baby brother and knows how to make me smile, even while getting on my nerves."

She reaches for the remote. "Makes me miss my sister."

My face softens. "I know, Piper. This will all be over soon."

"I hope so because right now, it's pure torture. I mean, not because of you. You're...well, you're the way you always are. I just miss my life and freedom."

"I'll try not to take that personally."

She chuckles. "Good. So, *Housewives of New Jersey* or *LA*?"

I snort at my choices. "Surprise me."

CHAPTER SEVEN

PIPER

DAY 9

I'VE NEVER WATCHED SO much TV in my life.

And I'm pretty sure I'll go blind if I stare at the screen a minute longer.

Though it's been nice to just binge-watch some reality TV, I also feel like my brain cells are slowly dying. Between the *Housewives of New Jersey* and looking up recipes in the books Easton brought, the weekend flew by without any news from the police. My stalker is still on the loose, and they don't know where he is.

To make matters worse, I'm going stir-crazy not being able to see what people are saying online. I've never gone this long without uploading a video. Even though some of my sponsored Instagram posts are pre-scheduled, the fact I'm not responding to comments or updating my Instagram stories is undoubtedly being noticed. It's unlike me not to be very active, so I can only imagine the rumors that are spreading.

Since Tristan allows me to use the patio, I go outside and

call Kendall. Though she's on her honeymoon, she always picks up when I call. I know they're having a great time, so I try not to interrupt her too much or keep her for long.

"Can you do me a favor and post something on my Instagram? I don't know what's being said so I'd like to at least explain where I am, well not where I *really* am, but that I'm taking a mental health break and won't be uploading anything for a bit. Something along those lines. Use one of my pics I've sent you."

"Are you sure that's a good idea?"

"It's gotta be better than radio silence. I'm sure people think I went into rehab or something."

Kendall chuckles. "Alright, I'm sure I can whip up something vague and perky. Should I say you're taking a social media break in the Caymans?"

"No!" I laugh. "Nowhere specific. I don't need the locals looking for me, then saying I was lying."

"Okay, good point. Anything else? How's Operation Get Tristan to Fall in Love with You going?"

"Pretty sure he thinks of me as an annoying younger sister he's not being paid enough to babysit."

Ryan barks out a laugh but is smart enough to keep his snarky comments to himself.

"From what Mom has told me, they haven't tracked the guy down yet, so it sounds like you might be there for a bit longer. Time to step up your game," Kendall says with a flirtatious tone. "Took two weeks for me to make Ryan fall in love with me."

"Don't start planning my wedding, geez," I say with an eye roll. "You and Ryan had a history. Tristan and I barely know each other."

"Alright, so maybe it'll take him three instead. That still gives you plenty of time."

"Don't hold your breath. At this point, I'd settle for his friendship. I'm bored and lonely. All I get from him is his judgy eyes and silent criticisms."

"He's probably trying to hold back inappropriate comments about how hot you are," Kendall says. "I like to think that's why Ryan was so quiet in the beginning."

"Don't feed her that bullshit," Ryan interjects, and I chuckle at his blunt honesty.

"Well, I think I've had enough of this pep talk. I'm gonna call Mom and then try to figure out what to do with the other twelve hours of the day."

"You'll be alright, sis. I love you, stay safe, and listen to Tristan," Kendall tells me.

"Yeah, yeah. Love you too. Bye!"

I chat with my mother, letting her know that Easton's been bringing us things. She reassures me all of this is temporary, and while I know that, it still feels like this will last forever.

Once we say goodbye, I head in and set my phone down on the coffee table. Tristan isn't on the couch anymore, and I don't see him in the kitchen, so I assume he's in his room. I walk to the bathroom, needing to wash my face, though I've been cleaning it nonstop because my entire body is one big sweat ball.

"Oh my God!" I scream when I walk in on Tristan. He's standing naked in the shower with a towel over his shoulders, but surprisingly the happy trail that leads to his cock isn't what catches my attention.

"Where's your leg?" I blurt out, immediately wanting to smack myself. "Shit, sorry. I didn't mean to walk in on you.

The door wasn't locked, and I thought you were in your room, and—you're an amputee?" I exclaim all at once.

Tristan releases the shower bar, then calmly wraps the towel around his waist as he stands on one foot. It's then I see a prosthesis outside the shower, and he must've been in the process of putting it on when I barged in.

"Yes, I am," he says. "If you want to get technical, I'm a right BKA, which stands for below the knee amputee."

I blink, staring at half his leg. "How can you balance on one foot like that?"

"Years of practice, it's normal for me."

I swallow hard, feeling my body heat with embarrassment for the way I reacted.

Finally, I meet his eyes. "How didn't I know this whole time? You walk and do everything completely normal."

"That's kind of the point of having a prosthetic. I did months of therapy and rehab to get to this point. It wasn't always this easy."

"When did you lose it?"

"Ten years ago."

"When you were overseas?" I ask.

He doesn't respond, just nods, which tells me he doesn't want to talk about it.

"Would you mind giving me some privacy?"

I step back, blinking out of my trance. "Of course, sorry." I shut the door behind me.

As I walk to my room, I think about the dozens of times he's had to push people away from me who got too close, or how he's had to run to keep up with me in crowds, and at my sister's wedding when he drew a gun and confronted my stalker. I have no doubt he would've been able to catch him had people not been in his way. The other security couldn't even keep up with him.

I don't know why I'm so shocked, but I guess I had this idea of what someone with a prosthetic would look like or how they'd walk, and Tristan doesn't fit any of those images. He's stood for hours at a time when we've been in public, sits normally, and moves around the kitchen flawlessly as he cooks. I literally had no clue.

Along with that revelation, I have a million questions. Does wearing it hurt? Can he keep it on twenty-four hours a day? He clearly doesn't shower with it, but...does he have sex with it on?

Obviously, he'd never answer that last question, so I won't bother asking, but it's definitely in the back of my mind. Call me curious.

Truthfully, I don't know much about amputees, so I probably looked stupid as hell as I gawked at his leg.

It took me off guard because I had no idea and never got the impression he had a setback. Perhaps that's proof I haven't been paying much attention to him, and his disdain toward me is actually valid.

"Piper." I hear his booming voice outside my room.

I open the door and stare at a fully-clothed Tristan, but this time, I gaze my eyes down his body and wonder what his prosthetic looks like on him.

"Are you hungry?" he asks calmly.

"Sure, but can I pick what we eat this time?"

He crosses his arms and narrows his eyes, then cautiously agrees. "Fine. But nothing over the top."

"Over the top is my middle name. Thought you knew that by now," I muse, walking past him, leading the way to the kitchen.

First, I pull out the sourdough bread, cheddar cheese, and the fresh tomato Easton actually brought. As soon as Tristan sees the ingredients, he shakes his head with a knowing smirk.

"It's so easy, even you can't screw it up," I tease him.

"If it's so easy, then why don't you make it?" He waves his arm, gesturing for me to go ahead.

I square my shoulders and stand tall. "Fine, I will."

It's not that I don't cook for myself. I'm just not the best at it. I usually get distracted and end up burning something.

"You might want to turn the burner down, or your bread is gonna burn in seconds," Tristan says before I've even buttered it.

"Are you going to be a back-seat cook? Because I'd rather you go sit somewhere and stop watching me."

"Watching you is my job."

I roll my eyes. "Well, you can *watch* me from the living room."

"I have a feeling I should be near just in case a fire breaks out."

"Wow, you really have no faith in me." I slap the bread down in the pan and place the cheese and tomato on it before setting the other piece on top.

"I have faith that you're not very skilled in the kitchen."

I look over my shoulder to scowl at him as he gives me a cocky smirk. I meet it with a devilish grin of my own.

"That's fine. I'm skilled in other areas to make up for it," I taunt.

Our eyes lock together, and for a moment, I think he might ask me to elaborate, but before he can, the smoke detector blares, and my attention is brought back to the stove where smoke has taken over.

"Shit!" I take the towel and wave it around. Seconds later, Tristan takes the pan off the burner before turning it off. He grabs the towel from my hand and waves it under the detector.

My breathing picks up as he frantically opens the patio door to try to clear the house.

"Are you okay?" He stands in front of me, placing his palms on my shoulders. The temperature in the room grows hotter, but not because of the burnt food.

"Besides proving I'm a horrible cook? Yes."

"It's okay. I'll take care of this." He pats my arm, then cleans up.

I hate that he has to *take care of it* like I'm an incompetent child. He probably didn't mean it that way, but that's how it made me feel.

Taking a seat at the breakfast bar, I watch him move flawlessly around the kitchen as he remakes my sandwich. I stare at his leg, wondering how it feels to walk on a prosthetic and how he looks so natural.

"You have questions," he states in his deep baritone, but it's without judgment.

My gaze runs up his body, and I realize he caught me staring. I swallow hard and sit up straighter.

There's one question in particular that I'm curious about, and while I doubt he'll answer, I'm going for it. "How do you have sex?"

He blinks at me, his deadpan expression not giving his thoughts away. Out of all the questions in the world, I don't think he expected me to ask that.

"What?" he finally asks.

"Like do you keep it on? Do you take it off? How…do you have sex being an amputee?"

Tristan turns around, facing the stove, then returns with my sandwich. He hands over the plate, and I thank him.

"Well, it's not much different. How do you have sex *not* being an amputee?"

Him spinning the question around was unexpected. My face heats, and I'm positive my cheeks are blood red.

"Umm...well." I chew on my bottom lip, trying to form words that won't make it obvious I haven't actually had sex. "I guess that's fair."

Tristan's eyes narrow as if he can hear my thoughts, and his lips twist with amusement.

"Shut up," I groan, picking up my sandwich, then taking a bite. "I can't help that it was my first thought when I saw you naked without a leg." I shrug, hoping he doesn't notice how flushed I am.

It wasn't just the leg that caught my eye, but *everything* below his waist.

"I have plenty of leg to use, I'm just missing below my knee, but regardless, everything down *there* still works as it should." There's a hint of something in his tone as if to say he's not restricted in *any* regard.

"Okay, well, my curiosity thanks you for appeasing me."

"No problem." He taps his knuckles on the counter. "If you need a sex education book, just let me know, and I'll add it to Easton's list."

My jaw drops at his taunting voice, and the fire in his eyes tells me that he's read between the lines.

I'm a virgin, and now he fucking knows it.

CHAPTER EIGHT

TRISTAN

DAY 10

ANOTHER SLEEPLESS NIGHT haunts me as I struggle with the pain, which can't be cured by surgery or pain meds. It's been my demise for the past decade.

It's after one in the morning, but I go through the process of putting on my prosthesis, then slip on my jeans and holster before walking downstairs. Almost every night is like clockwork, the pain wakes me up from a deep sleep, and I have to find ways to manage it so I can eventually go back to sleep.

Once I'm in the kitchen, I heat the kettle, then make a cup of tea. I typically drink it to help me relax. After I add some honey, I notice a glow coming from the living room. After Piper went to bed, I did a perimeter check, triple-checked that all the doors and windows were locked, then turned off everything.

Quietly, I set down my mug and pull out one of my guns. Stepping out of the kitchen, I walk to the living room and scan the area. The lamp next to the couch is on, but I don't see anything else out of the ordinary.

"Hey."

I spin around, pointing the barrel directly in Piper's face. She ducks, and I quickly lower it.

"Jesus Christ. What are you doing in here?" I holster the weapon and stare at her.

"Me? What are *you* doing? Other than trying to kill me."

"I was making tea when I noticed the light was on and wanted to make sure no one was in the house," I explain. "Why're you up?"

She shrugs. "I was restless. Decided to have a snack and read a little, then I had to use the bathroom. The next thing I see is you pointing a gun in my face."

"I'm sorry, but you caught me off guard. You should know better than to sneak up on me."

"Alright, next time, I'll scream your name at the top of my lungs," she deadpans, then focuses her attention on my bare chest. "You couldn't sleep either?"

"No, but I struggle most nights." I walk past her and grab my mug, then meet her on the couch.

"Have you thought about medication?" she asks.

"I take something when I'm not working, but it doesn't help with the pain."

Her expression falls as she glances down at my leg. "Are you hurting right now?"

"Yes, it's phantom pain. Mostly happens when I'm not wearing my prosthetic, so sometimes it helps when I put it on and walk around. Kinda tricks my brain and makes it stop temporarily."

"So, it's not a physical discomfort?"

"It's all neurological. I feel throbbing, tingles, and aches in the part of my leg that I no longer have, usually my toes or foot. Oftentimes, my foot feels like it's being crushed or stabbed and even like it's on fire. Sometimes my ankle too. It feels very real to me. My brain never figured out half of my leg was missing. So, I can't just swallow a few pills and make it go away."

"Wow…I never knew that happened. If you can't take anything for it, what do you do?"

"Besides taking a walk, I just wait it out. Smoking marijuana has been known to help, but I can't do that on the job. I'm always on call and can't risk being caught with it or not being trusted to do my work."

"I'm sorry. I can't imagine."

"I'd never wish it on anyone. I've learned to deal with it because I have no choice, but I honestly can't remember what it was like not to suffer with it."

"Tristan, I-I had no idea. You hide it so well. Have you seen any specialists to see if there's something new you haven't tried?"

"Yes, I've done everything. I take meds for nerve pain, which helps minimize it, but I'm on the max dosage. If I take any more, I risk destroying my liver and kidneys. I was told that if my brain didn't register that the limb was gone within the first year, it was unlikely it ever would. Most amputees experience some degree of phantom pain. Some people suffer so badly, they end their lives."

When I look into her eyes, I see them well with tears, and I hate that she's pitying me. I never want sympathy from anyone—I fought for my country, and I'll never regret that.

"Have you ever thought of…doing *that*?" she asks cautiously.

"No, I have too much survivor's guilt. I couldn't go

through with it, not when I was granted a second chance. My brothers died that day, and I'm determined to keep living for them."

This is the most I've ever opened up to Piper. Maybe I'm vulnerable because it's late, or maybe it's because Piper truly seems interested in knowing more about me, but I don't know how to feel about it either.

"Even after knowing you for half a year, I realize I don't know that much about you or who you are as a person. Guess I have a lot to learn."

"It'd take months, maybe years, to unravel all of me," I say with a grin. "There's a lot to unpack, and I don't particularly like talking about it."

She flashes me a sweet smile and nods. "You're so damn strong to be able to deal with everything so flawlessly. I get period cramps and am out for four days straight."

I chuckle. "I know. I utilized those days to stay off my prosthetic and let the bottom of my residual limb heal."

She tilts her head, and I know she's going to have even more questions. *Shit.*

"I thought it was healed?"

"Consistently using a prosthesis can wear down the skin and even skilled amputees need breaks. It gets red and inflamed, and the skin can tear or bruise. Kinda depends on how bad the injury was in the first place, but I experience all of it if I don't take time to let it repair itself."

"You should've said something sooner. You know you could've taken days off that you needed if you were in pain or you needed to rest. Why didn't you tell me?"

"Because you're my responsibility, and I'm fiercely protective of you. If I didn't show up one day and something happened to you, I'd live with even more guilt. I signed up for this knowing my schedule would be intense, and I've handled it just fine."

"Considering I didn't know about any of this until just now, I'd say you're right, but going forward, don't be too proud to let me know."

"I suspect once your stalker is caught, you won't need a bodyguard anymore."

"Oh…" She frowns as if that just dawned on her. "I guess you're right. But knowing my father, who knows. He sleeps better at night knowing I'm not alone in public."

I finish my tea, then get up to put my cup in the sink. "You've been a good distraction, and I'm not hurting nearly as bad, so I think I'm gonna try to go back to sleep."

"Really? Guess that means you should talk to me about yourself more often," she gloats.

"I wouldn't go that far," I muse. "But I would like for you to go back to bed too. I won't be able to sleep knowing you're down here alone."

She sighs. "Fine, if it'll make you happy."

Piper stands and walks up to me, merely inches away as if she can't get close enough. I fight the urge to wrap my arms around her and properly thank her for listening. Even though I don't like bringing up the skeletons in my closet, I don't mind her questions. She's never judgmental, always curious, and I adore that about her.

From the moment we met, I was attracted to her. Who wouldn't be? She's beautiful, and even though she can be superficial, her bubbly personality is contagious. If I could let my guard down more, I know we'd get along well. But I'm not here to be her friend. I can't get close and lose sight of what I was hired to do.

Perhaps if we'd met on different terms, things could be

different. But even then, Piper's young and has her whole life ahead of her. The very last thing she'd need is some older damaged guy weighing her down.

"Good night, see you in the morning," I tell her, motioning for her to go ahead of me.

As I follow her up the stairs, I can't resist staring at her ass, and I think she knows it too. Her little pajama shorts barely cover her, and she taunts me with every step she takes.

"Night," she calls out as she goes to her room.

If I wasn't already going to bed with a hard-on, the vision of her ass molded into my brain would've done the job.

"I can't believe you can watch this over and over," I grumble when the housewives get into another screaming match.

"You do too," she retorts.

"Because I go where you go," I remind her. I refuse to admit that the over-the-top drama is actually entertaining.

"You could be doing other things. Easton brought all those adult coloring books and magazines." She snickers.

"Yeah, maybe I'll save that for after dinner."

Piper snorts. "It's starting to feel like Groundhog's Day. When are they gonna catch Jack so we can go back home?"

"That reminds me. I should call in. Be right back." I stand, then go to the kitchen so I can talk to her dad in private.

"How is she?" Mr. Montgomery asks.

"Going stir-crazy, but overall, she's fine. Do you have any updates?"

"I hired a new private investigator who questioned his co-workers and doorman and found out he hasn't been at work or home in a week. They're tracking his credit cards for movement, but so far, they haven't located him. He's assumed to be on the run or hiding somewhere."

My heart drops, knowing it's not the news Piper wants to hear.

"He could be anywhere right now," I say.

"Correct. And until he's arrested, Piper must stay hidden."

"I understand, sir. I'm watching her every move and keeping the house secure."

"Good. As soon as we've got eyes on him, I'll let you know. He can't stay under the radar forever."

"Certainly hope not."

After hanging up, I start dinner and think about what will happen once we've returned to New York. My living arrangements are only temporary, and as soon as Piper's considered safe, I'll be looking for another job.

"Something smells good. What are you cooking?" Piper comes up behind me as I stir the sauce.

"Creamy garlic chicken," I reply, feeling her hot breath on my arm as she looks at the pan.

"Oh. I'll make the veggies."

Piper grabs a bag of broccoli from the freezer and pops it into the microwave. "Alright, well that was easy. Let me get the plates."

I snicker at how she attempts to help since her burnt grilled cheese incident yesterday.

Once the chicken is out of the oven, I add it to the sauce and let it simmer.

"So what'd my dad say?" she asks while setting the table.

I repeat everything he said, and she blows out a frustrated breath.

"If Jack's as techy and smart as you say, he probably knows how to stay off the grid while trying to track me down. Wouldn't it just be faster to lure him here and catch him with some extra backup? Then he can be arrested, and I can go back to living in the twenty-first century."

"Afraid not," I tell her. "We can't risk that. He could kill you before he's captured."

"If he wanted to hurt me, he could've at Kendall's wedding. He had no weapons," she states. "Maybe he's just using scare tactics to get my attention?"

"The death threats and vile photos tell me otherwise. Also, we don't know if he had weapons that night. No one caught him to check."

Piper grabs the veggies, then screams, dropping the bag on the floor. "Shit, that's hot."

I rush over and gently take her wrist, then lead her to the sink. "Put it under cold water."

As I hold her hand under the stream, I rub the pad of my thumb over her palm.

"I think I'm okay," she says softly after a few moments. I meet her gaze, and a thousand sparks fly between us.

Fuck. I can't cross those lines or give her the wrong idea.

After I turn off the water, I check her hand. "You're a hazard in the kitchen. You need to be more careful."

"I didn't know it would be that hot," she explains. "But yes, you're right. That's what I get for trying to help."

I hand her a towel, and she dries her hand. "Go sit. I'll finish."

Once she's settled at the table, I bring her a plate full, then sit across from her.

"When I'm back home, I'm signing up for cooking classes," she blurts out, and I immediately laugh.

"Which celebrity chef will be featured on your channel?"

She narrows her eyes and glares at me. "I wasn't going to film it, jackass. I was just telling you I've realized I need to learn some basics."

"That's an understatement," I tease.

"Hey, it's not my fault. My parents set me up for failure. Imagine waking up every morning to a gourmet meal served by a personal chef and a housekeeper who picked up every mess. I wasn't taught basic life skills. When I was older, it was a culture shock to find that not everyone lived that way. Now that I live on my own, I'm willing to try new things and only have a housekeeper come once a week. Most trust fund babies don't even bother. They'll pay someone for literally *everything*."

"So why did you start a YouTube channel? It's not like you needed the money or sponsorships," I ask the question I'd been wondering since day one.

"Because I wanted something that was just mine, something I earned and worked for, a passion project that I started from the ground up. Sure, my name gave me a foundation, but my content keeps them watching. That's something only I can claim."

"I've watched a few of your videos," I admit.

"Only a few?" She arches a brow.

"I don't really need makeup advice, fashion hauls, or to keep up with the latest trends."

She rolls her eyes, stabbing a piece of chicken with her fork. "So which ones do you watch?"

I contemplate lying but don't because we're being open and honest.

"Your day in the life vlogs are my favorite. They show more of who you are versus the act you put on in the others."

"For the last time, I'm not acting. I'm just showing off sponsored products, so I might exaggerate a little, but—"

"You haven't talked about a single brand you've worked with while we've been here. In fact, you've looked more like your true self these past ten days than ever before."

She glowers as if what I said was an insult, but it's quite the opposite.

"What look is that exactly?"

"This *no makeup, messy bun, leggings, and T-shirt* look. You're comfortable in your own skin, more relaxed, and you laugh like you mean it. There's not an ounce of fakeness on you." And it's driving me absolutely fucking crazy. The urge to drink her in every time she walks in the room gets stronger with each passing day.

I think back to that first day she filmed a tour of the house and talked like she was living her best life when she'd been complaining moments before.

"You wouldn't understand. If I act unhappy about something, I'm immediately criticized and called ungrateful. There's an expectation that comes with being in my family."

"Yeah, I have no idea what that's like," I deadpan. "Honestly, I may not be at your level, but I live with expectations too. Every single day."

I lower my eyes, cutting my chicken, and think about every man we lost that day in the explosion that blew off part of my leg. If I openly complained about the pain, people would think I'm ungrateful to be alive. They like to associate the two together when the two can co-exist.

We finish eating in silence, and after she puts her plate in the sink, she announces she's going to take a bath.

I take that time to clean up the kitchen and place the leftovers in the fridge for tomorrow. As I rinse the dishes, I replay our conversation. I suspect I'm the only person in her life who doesn't feed her lines of bullshit. Then again, most of her friends and fans are in their early twenties and don't have a clue about the real world.

"Hey, Tristan!" I hear Piper calling from the bathroom.

I tap on the door before opening it. "You okay?"

Piper's covered by bubbles but pokes a foot out as she plays with the suds. "Yeah, I just forgot a towel. Would you mind grabbing me one, please?"

"Sure."

I take one from the linen closet, then set it down on the counter. "You need anything else?"

Her chest moves up and down, every inch revealing more and more of her as she contemplates my question.

"No, I'm good. Thanks."

I close the door behind me, then wait for her in the living room. As I aimlessly flip through a magazine, I make a mental note of what I need Easton to bring when he returns.

Footsteps patter on the floor, and when I look over, Piper's walking out completely wet and naked.

"What the fuck are you doing?" I growl out as she walks closer.

"I forgot my phone on the coffee table." She flashes a Cheshire cat smirk that tells me all I need to know.

"Why are you naked?" I demand, forcing my eyes above her neck.

"You only gave me *one* towel, so I made an executive decision to use it for my hair." She shrugs as if it's the most logical solution she could come up with.

"You didn't ask for two," I remind her.

"Oops." She takes her phone, then spins around, and this time, my eyes do wander. Down her back and to her hips, then to her curvy ass as she walks away.

Every sexy inch of her is taunting me, a forbidden treat I can't eat. She's dangling it in front of me, torturously showing me what's off-limits.

Piper Montgomery is a temptation I can never give in to— no matter how badly I want to break the rules.

CHAPTER NINE

PIPER

DAY 11

I CAN'T BELIEVE I'm still in Florida. When I arrived, I thought they'd find Jack within a week, but it's been eleven days now and still no sighting of him. I've tried to keep myself busy, but I'm growing bored.

As soon as the sun rose, I woke up because I was uncomfortable and hot. I lay in bed for a few hours staring at the ceiling as I replayed the conversation Tristan and I had last night. His words have been on repeat in my mind, and I still can't believe I wasn't aware of any of his struggles and what he deals with on a daily basis. I have so much respect for him.

Eventually, I grab my backpack and go downstairs. Tristan is reading in the living room. He gives me a head nod and goes back to his book. After I make a cup of coffee, I power on my laptop.

My desktop is full of screenshots, pointless memes, and random articles I downloaded. Going through all of that took four hours, but I deleted over fifty gigs of crap. I'm going to try to do a better job of it, but it's hard to stay on top of. My days are usually so packed with recording and editing that any downtime is a luxury I use for sleep.

After eating leftover chicken and veggies for lunch, I ask Tristan if I can sit in the backyard.

He narrows his eyes, and I'm convinced he'll say no as he has every other time.

"Okay, but if I see anyone walking on the beach or acting suspicious, back inside we go."

"Yay! Thank you!" I grin wide, grabbing my notebook. He stands and joins me.

I suck in the fresh air and love the sound of the waves crashing on the shore. Once I'm settled, I flip to a blank page and get to work.

"What are you writing over there?" he asks after about ten minutes of me scribbling away in my notebook.

"Video ideas for when I can start recording and posting again."

He tilts his head and glances at my sheet. I turn it so he has a better view. "Wait, you actually plan them out?"

I snicker. "You think I'm good enough to just wing it every single day?"

He laughs. "Yeah."

"Thanks for the confidence, but actually no. It takes a lot more than just picking up a camera."

"Interesting." By his tone, he actually sounds intrigued. Tristan's eyes scan the beach as an older woman collecting seashells passes in the distance. He tenses, and I see his hand go toward one of his guns, but then he relaxes.

I speak up, bringing his attention back to me. "So I come up with a few titles, then check their searchability online. See if they'll rank or trend. Then I outline the video with bullet points. If it's a get ready with me, I usually have a sponsor. But if it's like a vlog, I try to tell an underlying story so it's not just random clips."

"That's smart. Probably why I like them so much," he says.

Knowing Tristan has watched my videos has heat rushing through me, but I push those electrical currents to the side. "I learned a long time ago that if I can teach my subscribers something, add in a little spice or drama, then end with a positive note, they respond well. The longer they watch, the more money I make."

"How many have you outlined so far?"

I bite my lip and turn the pages in my spiral. "Since we've been here? I've written down about fifteen ideas. That's about two weeks' worth of content."

"See, being here wasn't a complete waste of your time."

"I guess you could say that, but I'll have more than enough catching up to do once I'm back. I'll have to hit it hard and hope the algorithm doesn't hate me."

"I'm sure you'll be fine."

When Tristan's phone rings, he immediately picks it up. His back straightens, and his jaw clenches as he paces in front of the lawn chair.

I'm starting to sweat because there's hardly any breeze, so I let him know I'm going inside. He gives me a head nod and continues his conversation.

Five minutes later, Tristan enters as I'm sitting at the table chugging water. The humidity here is deadly, and the last thing I need is to get dehydrated and have to be rushed to the emergency room. Apparently, it's very easy to do in Florida.

I spend the better half of the afternoon planning, lost in my own world. Eventually, Tristan begins pulling things out of the kitchen cabinets. Curious, I sit on the barstool and watch him.

"What are you making?" I ask.

He gives me a side grin. "My mama's lasagna."

"Homemade?"

"Yeah. Come on, I'll teach you."

I hop off the stool and wash my hands before standing beside him. He smells so damn good, and I have to force myself not to move closer. Tristan glances at me. "Did you hear me?"

I shake my head. "Sorry, I got distracted."

I leave out the part that he was to blame as he wipes down the counter.

"So you'll crack those two eggs into the bowl and stir them together vigorously with this fork." He hands it to me.

I carefully grab them and tap one against the side of the counter. It doesn't do the job, so I smash it a little harder until it breaks open and pieces of the shell go inside the bowl. "Shit."

"It's okay. Just pick them out," he tells me patiently.

"You know I'm terrible at this. Not sure why you keep giving me chances," I admit, making sure I get every piece of rogue shell out of the mix.

"It's because I don't give up on people. I'll teach you everything I know." Tristan winks, and butterflies swarm in my stomach.

I do the other one without messing it up, then vigorously mix them together.

Tristan opens the flour and pulls out a huge measuring cup, then fills it nearly full.

"I'm going to slowly add this in your bowl. Keep stirring." He moves closer, his arm touching mine as he incorporates the flour.

"We're about to use our hands," he says when I have a big

soft ball of dough in the bowl. "You can dump it on the counter."

"Really?"

He laughs, sprinkling flour on the flat surface. "Yeah, go ahead."

After I do, he places his strong hands in the dough and shows me how to knead it. He takes my hand, flipping it over, and runs his finger along my palm.

"You'll use this part and push down." Tristan meets my eyes, and I get lost in them.

There are so many unspoken words that I can't be the only one who feels what's streaming between us. He pulls away, splitting the dough in two. The way he works it with his big, strong hands makes me jealous as hell, wishing he was touching my body instead.

"We'll do this until it's silky smooth." The rasp in his voice has me squeezing my legs together.

"See," he finally says after about five minutes. "It's ready."

"Amazing," I say as he wraps it in plastic and places it in the fridge. "Oh, why'd you do that?"

"To let it rest. If you don't, it'll be a disaster. We've had enough of those in the kitchen this trip."

I playfully swat at him, and he chuckles. "I had no idea so much went into lasagna. Makes me appreciate each time I've eaten it."

"Absolutely. Kinda funny how that works. It's impossible to understand without getting the full picture." Silence rings out. That sentence has so many more meanings than I'm sure he intended. "Time to start on our tomato sauce."

"I don't know what I did to deserve such a fancy meal."

Tristan bursts into laughter. "You really have been in isolation for way too long."

I give him a toothy grin. "Maybe you're right."

He chops onion and garlic, then swirls olive oil in a hot skillet before throwing it in. I take the spatula and move it around so it doesn't burn. Then he adds the meat. Once it's fully cooked and the house smells amazing, I turn off the stove.

"We need to make the ricotta. If you could pull it out of the fridge and add one egg, I'll finish up the sauce."

He wipes his forehead with the back of his hand, then starts adding different cans of tomatoes. I love watching the way he works in the kitchen, and I'm completely mesmerized by him.

"Wanna taste?" he offers me the mixing spoon.

"Yes!" I lean forward, my eyes magnetized to his as I try it. All I want to do is take the spoon from his hand and lick it. "This is...*orgasmic*."

Tristan nearly chokes, then puts the cover on the finished meat sauce.

"Wanna grab the dough from the fridge?"

"Sure," I say, then hand it to him. After he plops it down on the counter, he offers me the rolling pin.

"I just..." I grab each side and make a rolling motion.

He smirks. "Yep."

I start in the middle but realize it's too hard to squish, so I move to the edges. Tristan patiently watches me and randomly sprinkles more flour on the counter when the dough sticks. When it's finally flat, I stand back in amazement at what I've accomplished.

"I'll let you do the honors." He hands me a knife. "Cut them about three inches wide."

"You're sure about this?" I ask hesitantly.

"Yeah, just go slow and keep your fingers out of the way."

Eventually, I have several twelve-inch-long strips. Tristan grabs a pot of water and fills it with water.

"We're boiling them?"

"Sometimes, you're really adorable."

"*Sheltered* is what you mean."

"Or spoiled," he adds with a laugh.

I grab some flour and throw it at him. It splatters across his shirt. Immediately, he flicks some right back at me. White dust flies all over the kitchen as we're laughing and running from each other. He catches me and places his hands gently on my waist. We're both dusted with white powder, and right now, I want nothing more than to feel his soft lips brush against mine.

I swallow hard, peering into his green eyes.

He clears his throat. "We should probably finish so we can get it into the oven."

"Yeah," I whisper, confused by the emotions swirling through me.

Carefully, I grab the strips one by one and set them in the water. We wait around in the kitchen for them to boil. Tristan reaches over and wipes flour from my face. It's one of those moments that has my heartstrings fluttering, and I'm almost convinced he can hear it. I lick my lips, ready to say something, but he creates space before I can. Instantly, I feel the loss of his closeness, but I saw how he looked at me because I'm certain I was looking at him the same way.

"Flour is everywhere." He laughs

Tristan guides me through the rest of the steps and finally slides the glass pan of our homemade lasagna into the oven.

"This is my favorite recipe, though it takes a bit of time."

"I think it's quickly become mine too," I admit, the words

falling out of my mouth. Being with him like this is a memory I'll treasure forever.

I'm confused by what I feel for him, knowing it's not ideal to cross the line with my bodyguard, but I can't help the way my heart beats faster every time he's close. Especially as I'm learning who Tristan really is.

"It reminds me of being a kid and helping my mom in the kitchen without a care in the world. It was a simpler time back then."

"It's great that you have fond memories and traditions like that. I can't say I have many when it comes to my parents. Growing up, I had nannies who practically raised me as my parents controlled me with rules and expectations. Minus the nanny, and things are still the same. It helped Kendall and I bond at least."

His expression softens. "I'm sorry. That kind of breaks my heart a little."

I shrug. "I guess the reality is money can't buy love, you know? You can purchase everything you want in the world, but something's always still missing." I let out a deep breath, realizing how much truth just came out. "I'm sorry."

He shakes his head. "Don't ever be sorry to share your feelings with me, Piper. Ever."

"Thanks."

We sit at the table, adding pieces to the puzzle until the timer buzzes.

"Oh my God, it's ready?" I stand, excited to see the final product.

"Yep!" He grabs the oven mitts, then sets the hot pan on the stovetop. I stand next to him, looking at how the cheese bubbles on top.

"Let's cut into it," I say eagerly.

Tristan chuckles. "Gotta let it cool for like ten minutes. Then it's all yours."

"I am *not* a patient person."

He glances over at me and smirks. "That's the truth."

I playfully elbow him, and he pretends I punched the wind out of him. We both laugh, and though I'm not sure what's going on between us right now, I can't say I'm disappointed.

Over the past week and a half, Tristan has knocked down a few of my walls, and I've unraveled some of his past. Progress —it's something we haven't had until now.

CHAPTER TEN

TRISTAN

DAY 12

I SUCK in a deep breath as I make a perimeter check outside. Yesterday when I spoke to Mr. Montgomery, he reiterated that Jack was still MIA and to triple-check that the house was secure. For all I know, he could be on his way to Florida.

While we've been in hiding and Piper's been off social media, there's still the potential that Jack can find her. We've done everything possible to keep her location a secret, but we don't know his intelligence level, so I'm not taking any chances.

I spend the rest of the morning reading while Piper records a video about learning how to make homemade lasagna. I smile with amusement at her excitement. I try to tune her out so I can focus on my book, but it's almost impossible when she's gushing so hard.

We eat leftovers for lunch, then she gets on her laptop. Meanwhile, I bury myself on the couch with one of the thrillers my brother brought me. I've already read the other two.

An hour or so later, I hear Piper rummaging around in the kitchen. Moments later, she plops down on the opposite end with a bottle of whiskey in her hand.

"Uh, where did you get that?"

She snickers. "I found it in one of the cabinets."

I can't help but laugh when she twists off the cap and takes a swig.

"I have no idea how old that is, and I'm not sure it's a good idea for you to be chugging it like it's water."

"I'd google it, but you know…no internet and all of that." She waves her hand around.

I look at the time on my phone. "It's two in the afternoon."

Piper shrugs. "Oh well, it's five o'clock somewhere."

She takes another gulp and wiggles her body afterward.

"Yeah, that Wild Turkey is going to do you in."

"Listen, I'm old enough to drink and can handle my alcohol just fine." She repositions her body and puts her legs on the couch until her feet are nearly in my lap. It's then I notice how smooth her skin is and how goddamn beautiful she looks in this lighting. Well, really any time, but it's not something I can ever say aloud.

"Let's play a game…" she suggests. After every sentence she speaks, I swear she tips the bottle to her lips. "A *drinking* game."

With a smirk, I meet her eyes. "I'll play, but I won't be partaking in ten-year-old whiskey shots or *any* alcohol."

She sticks out her bottom lip and pouts.

"I have to be responsible, Piper. In case some psycho finds us and you need protecting. But…I'll play a game."

"I guess I'll take what I can get." Piper stands and slightly stumbles before laughing at herself. She carries the bottle with her and walks to the game closet.

While she takes her time reading the titles out loud, I know she's never played any of them. It's like being locked up with someone who's been sheltered their entire life, and in an unconventional way, she has.

"This is the one." She returns to the couch with Sorry!, a game I haven't played since I was a kid. This time, she sits right next to me, the warmth of her bare skin taunting me. The sweet smell of her hair is intoxicating, but I try to ignore how my body reacts to it.

Opening the box, I set up the board. "Pick your color."

"I'll be red," she tells me, then I explain the rules.

"We should sit on the floor so we have more room."

"Fine with me."

She moves everything in front of the fireplace, and we get comfortable around it.

"So, just to make sure I've got this right…if one of us lands in the same space as the other, then the pawn returns to start. The first one to get all their colors to home base wins."

"Correct."

"Got it. You can jump and bump. I guess now it's time to add a little spice."

I pop a brow at her.

"You said you won't be drinking but…"

"I'm not sure I like where this is going."

She flashes a mischievous grin. "How about each time we're bumped out of our spot, you lose a piece of clothing. And since I'm drinking, I'll also take a shot."

"You're stacking the game where we'll be buck-ass naked by the end of it, especially because taking your opponent out is the goal."

"Exactly," she slurs.

"Clothing stays on," I state.

"We'll see about that." She takes a card and moves her red pawn onto the board.

Piper's smiling and having a good time as we play. All of our pawns are on the board when I draw a Sorry! card, which means one of her pieces goes back to start.

"No fair!" she says, and I knock the one closest to being in the safe zone.

She chugs, then takes off her shirt.

"Clothing on," I remind her.

"Not happening." She throws the material to the side.

I try to keep my eyes above her neck, but it's so damn hard when her breasts are nearly falling out of the bra that is nothing more than a decoration. Her perky pink nipples are at full attention, and if we were two different people, I'd lay her down on the carpet and worship her the way she wants.

I swallow hard as my throat goes dry. Right now, she's purposely pushing my buttons, trying to get me to crack, but I refuse.

Piper leans forward to grab a card, looking up and meeting my eyes with a devious smirk on her lips.

Goddammit.

She moves her pawn two spots. I draw another card, praying I don't land in the same spot as her, but I'm not so lucky.

"Oops, looks like I'm going back home," she mutters as she climbs to her feet. Piper sways as she bends over, sliding her jean shorts down, then kicks them off. The little devil is wearing a thong. It's see-through, just like her bra, and leaves *nothing* to the imagination.

I keep my eyes on the board, not giving her the satisfaction of knowing she's driving me fucking crazy.

"You like?" she asks, spinning around and giving me a view of her plump ass cheeks. My eyes wander down her body, and I notice she's completely bare between her legs. I'd be a fucking liar if I said I wasn't struggling with my willpower to stay away.

"Sit," I snap between gritted teeth. She chuckles, then takes another swig.

I try to act normal, like we're playing a children's game, and she's not in my head. Piper watches me as I clench my jaw. This game needs to end now, and the sooner, the fucking better.

We go through the motions of drawing cards, and when I knock another one of hers off, she reaches behind her and removes her bra.

"Piper," I growl. "Put it back on, right now."

She crawls toward me, and I lean back, trying to create space, but fail. Her lips are mere inches from mine. "Keep pretending you don't find me attractive, Tristan. But I know the truth."

She moves in, and I grab her shoulders, stopping her lips from touching mine. I'm not sure I'd be able to stop myself if she made a move. This is dangerous territory.

"You've had too much to drink," I tell her, smelling it on her breath, and she returns to her spot. The pieces are scattered, but I declare her the winner to end the game.

"It's not over yet," she says, her words carrying sexual undertones that I can't escape.

I try to snap myself out of her spell as I shove everything into the box. "You had more pieces in the safe zone than me. You won," I explain.

She bites her bottom lip, grabs her bra, and snaps it on.

I can't open Pandora's box and discover what the fuck she's talking about even though, deep down, I know. I need to ignore my attraction to her no matter how badly I want to explore it.

"You should probably sleep off the alcohol before dinner. A few more shots and you'll be a sloppy drunk."

She flashes me a stubborn glare, picks up the bottle, then downs it.

I give her a disapproving look. "You're gonna regret that."

"We'll see. But you know, I think I will go upstairs and lie in my bed. Wanna join me?" she taunts.

"No."

"Can't say I didn't offer," she sing-songs, sashaying up the stairs and leaving her clothes on the living room floor.

"Hold the railings," I shout when she wobbles.

She giggles as she trips over herself.

"Jesus Christ," I mutter.

Instead of watching her struggle or waiting for her to break something, I help her.

She stops at the doorway of her room and studies my lips with hooded eyes. "I really wish you'd consider loosening up more."

I can't cross the line. I can't touch her, no matter what.

Those words are on repeat in my head. It could be disastrous for us both, and there's no telling how long we'll be here. Not only is it unprofessional on my part but it could also make things awkward between us.

"Too bad you won't, though." She stumbles forward, and I catch her before she face-plants. I cup her cheek, almost allowing myself to give in to what our bodies want. Our lips are close, too damn close, and her breath hitches.

Before I do something stupid, I step back and clear my throat. "Have a good nap."

"Thanks." She lowers her eyes, and I watch as she goes into her room.

I go downstairs and run my fingers through my hair, trying to get a grip on reality. Images of Piper's beautiful body and the way she was eye fucking me haunt me as I remind myself *why* I can't go there. Letting out a harsh breath, I adjust my hard cock that's begging to come out and play. I didn't realize something as harmless as playing a board game could go from G-rated to NC-17 so quickly, or I'd have never suggested we play.

After I decide to make fish and veggies for dinner, I check on Piper to make sure she's okay. When my foot hits the top of the stairs, I hear heavy breathing and low whimpers. Her door is cracked open, so I quietly walk toward it.

"Fuck," she whisper-hisses, and when I peek inside, blood rushes straight to my dick. Piper's completely naked on the bed with her back arched as she finger-fucks herself. Her mouth is wide as she pants and moans, moving her fingers from her pussy to her clit.

I shouldn't be watching, and I tell myself to leave, but I'm too entranced by her. I can tell she's close by her unsteady breathing, but before she comes, she places her fingers in her mouth. Piper returns to her clit with slow and meticulous motions, allowing her orgasm to build again before she stops. Piper's a fucking minx as she teases herself.

My eyes fall to her pink nipples while the sound of her pants and hard breathing increases.

"Tristan, yes…" she whispers.

My heart beats faster as she moans my name.

"Fuck, that's so good. Right there," she continues. There's

no way she knows I'm here because her eyes have been closed since I came upstairs.

Right now, she's getting off to thoughts of me, and I'm two seconds away from bursting in to help her get there.

She inserts two fingers, and I can tell how wet she is just by the sound of them thrusting in and out.

My dick throbs as she finally groans out through an orgasm. Her body convulses as her back straightens, and she comes all over her fingers.

Guilt floods through me for witnessing something so private and intimate, but I couldn't help it. Once I saw her, I was frozen in place. Finally, I go to my room and carefully close the door.

I sit on my bed and close my eyes. Images flood in of her touching herself as I unbutton and unzip my jeans. My dick is hard and throbbing, begging for release. I roughly grab myself, stroking to the thoughts of Piper—her little nipples, her perfect pussy, the sound of her whispering my name.

I pick up my pace, growing more eager and rough as I violently stroke my shaft. I need to come so goddamn bad it hurts. With my back plastered on the mattress, I try to hold back my grunts as my muscles tense.

Fuck, fuck, fuck.

The explosion rips through me as I come all over my hand. I try to steady my breathing so she doesn't hear the orgasm coursing through me. Five minutes pass before I can grasp reality and pull my pants back up.

I've never come so hard in my life, and there's only one woman to blame.

CHAPTER ELEVEN

PIPER

DAY 13

It's July first, which means I've been stuck inside for nearly two weeks. Not being able to read the comments on the post Kendall made is making me twitch. Luckily, we're chatting today, and I plan to find out everything she knows.

"Hey, sis, how ya holding up?" she asks in a cheerful tone.

I sit outside and huff, ignoring the mild hangover I woke up with this morning. I'm not about to mention the embarrassing stunt I pulled yesterday. Tristan was a proper gentleman while I stripped down nearly naked and drank too much. I could barely look him in the eyes this morning as he served breakfast and asked how I slept.

With my hand between my legs, thinking of him.

"I'm losing my damn mind. What are people saying about me online?"

"Pipes, you don't need to worry about childish gossip. Take this time for a refresh, a mental health break—like you told everyone—so—"

"Kendall. Tell me, *please*," I plead.

She blows out a breath. "Fine, but it's not good."

I squeeze my eyes shut, then inhale. "Just spit it out."

"The main one is that you're hiding a pregnancy."

"What? That's it? That'll be easy to argue when I return without a baby."

"Yeah, but they'll just make up something else to explain it. But..."

"What else?"

"They're saying you were secretly screwing your bodyguard. Apparently, Mom and Dad were so embarrassed and upset that they sent you away while they *got rid* of Tristan."

"Oh my God, that's ridiculous. They're acting like Dad's the leader of the Mafia." I pinch the bridge of my nose. "Why would getting pregnant be so scandalous anyway? I'm twenty-one."

"Allegedly because the Montgomery *princess* settled for someone below her class, and that's something to gossip about," Kendall says with a groan. "Their opinions are off base and don't matter, which is why you shouldn't let it get to you."

"I'm not."

"I know you and how you overanalyze what the haters say. Internet trolls just want something to talk about."

She's right, but it still stings when people gossip about my personal life. Regardless, it frustrates the hell out of me that I can't prove them wrong or defend my damn self.

"I should be allowed to be offline for a couple of weeks without these ridiculous rumors," I grind out. "It sucks that I can't throw how wrong they are in their faces."

"Who cares what they think? They'll move onto something else in a day or two."

"You're right. But who knows, I could've eloped by then," I deadpan.

Kendall chuckles. "You better not. Mom and Dad will kill you both."

"Trust me, Tristan's not interested."

"I find that really hard to believe. If he knew you were an option and were interested in him the same way, there's no way he'd reject you."

"There's something I just learned about Tristan that you don't know," I say cautiously, wondering if I should tell her.

"Huh? What? He's a spy? An undercover agent? Works for the CIA?"

I snort, knowing she can keep a secret. "You're reading too many romance novels. No, he lost his leg when he was overseas. He's an amputee."

"What? Seriously? You can't even tell."

"I know, which is why I had no idea."

"How'd you find out?"

I chew on my bottom lip before spilling the beans. "I accidentally walked in on him in the bathroom as he was drying off. I saw his prosthetic."

"I'd say you saw *a lot* more than that…"

I burst out laughing. "Oh, I did…He's hard *everywhere*."

"Jesus, Piper! You looked, you dirty virgin."

I roll my eyes. "Yeah, he's aware of that too."

"Do I even want to know how that came up?"

I scratch my cheek. "Nope."

"Well, it sounds like some of those rumors might actually be facts, at least the banging your bodyguard part. But if you want to give me a niece or nephew, I'm down for that too."

"Good lord. You're as bad as Mom." I grunt.

"Yeah, well, now Dad's gonna be on my ass to populate the Montgomery bloodline," she exaggerates in a deep, manly tone.

"Ew. Maybe I'll get an IUD just to spite him."

Kendall chuckles. "Yeah right. But you already know our parents approve of Tristan, so…"

"To protect me, not pop my cherry."

"You sure? Because he looks like a man who knows what he's doing…"

"Kendall! You're a married woman."

"Ryan knew what he was getting into. Plus, I'm talking about *for you*, not me."

"Well, you were the one who said older men are where it's at, so if Mom and Dad have a heart attack, I'll blame you."

"Deal. Now go experience second base."

"You bitch!" I laugh. "You act like I haven't done *anything*."

"Well, I don't know. You never give me any juicy details, yet you always want them from me."

"Not anymore, now that you've got that ring on your finger."

"Well, I want them from you, just remember that. No matter who it is."

"Duly noted."

"Alright, I better go. I have a ton of work to catch up on. Try to have fun while you're there."

"Yeah, yeah…" I grumble. "Call you in a couple of days."

"Bye, love you."

"Love you too."

After we hang up, I go inside and find Tristan.

"How's Kendall?" he asks.

"She's good." I let out a deep breath.

"What's up?"

"There are rumors about me hiding because I'm pregnant," I tell him, leaving out the part that he's the one who allegedly knocked me up.

"Oh. Well isn't it going to be obvious when you go back *not* pregnant?"

"I wish it were that easy. Bad press isn't good press in my situation. Not when it comes to YouTube and being targeted by cancel culture."

"Sorry, I don't know anything about that. But who cares?"

I give him a flat expression, and he shrugs, knowing damn well what people think of me is part of my career.

Needing to change the subject, I ask, "Can we please go to the beach today? My tan is fading, and I need to see the sun for a little bit. Even just ten minutes."

"Not yet."

I blow out a defeated breath with slouched shoulders as I sit at the breakfast bar. I could film another vlog, but I haven't felt inspired to pick up my camera lately. After Tristan commented about how I'm pretending to be someone I'm not for the sake of views, I haven't wanted to prove him right.

"I'm going to lose my sanity," I mutter as I bang my forehead against the counter.

Tristan's hand catches me before I can slam it down again.

"If you keep that up, you'll give yourself brain damage."

"Good. Maybe it'll numb my boredom."

"I see we've entered the melodramatic phase of isolation. Let's find something to do."

I sit up excitedly. "Go to the beach?"

"No."

I frown. "Then what do you suggest?"

"We could play another game? There are a few more in the closet."

"Are you saying you want to play Strip Sorry! again?" I taunt, surprised he brought it up after yesterday.

He crosses his arms. "No. You don't play fair."

I gasp. "That's not true! You just didn't like *my* rules. Today, they'll be different."

"Alright," he says hesitantly as if he doesn't trust me.

"Okay. Let's go." I jump off the stool and move to the living room, then grab the Sorry! box from the coffee table. Yesterday, he was noticeably trying to hold his willpower, and today, I'm going to see if it finally snaps.

"If you get bumped back to start, you have to do whatever the other person says," I explain as I set up everything. "And when your piece makes it home to the safe zone, you'll give a demand."

"Anything?" He raises a brow.

"*Anything*," I reiterate. "Unless you have limits?"

"Do you?" His lips tilt up just slightly on one side.

"Nope. I'm all in."

"Alright. Well, since this is *your* game, I'll be all in too."

"Great. Ladies first then."

I draw a card and get one, so I take my pawn out and move it. We go back and forth until I land where he is and send him back to start.

"So, what do I have to do?" he asks with a cocky grin.

If he thinks I'm going to take it easy on him, he's a fool. I'm done waiting and am going straight for what I want.

"You have to kiss me."

His lack of reaction scares me for a moment before he leans forward, grabs my hand, then kisses my knuckles.

My face scrunches. "That's the best you've got?"

"You didn't specify where I had to kiss you."

Motherfucker.

"Okay, fair point." Next time, I'll be crystal clear.

His next card is an eleven, which can be used to move eleven spaces or switch places with an opponent. He decides to bump me back to start and take my spot.

"Guess it's your turn to tell me what to do," I say, hiding my nervousness.

"Think this might be the first time you'll actually do something for me," he muses, and I roll my eyes.

"Har har. Now what is it?"

"Give me a foot massage."

"What?" My jaw drops. "Are you serious?"

"Yep, and I want it with lotion," he adds with a devilish smirk that I'd like to smack off his handsome face. "There's some in the bathroom."

Groaning, I stand and search for the bottle. It's some kind of medicated shit that smells like coconut.

When I return, Tristan has his leg on the coffee table with his jeans rolled up and his sock and shoe are off. The smug bastard leans back on the couch with his hands behind his head. When our eyes meet, he wiggles his toes and tells me he's ready.

Deciding to play him at his own game, I kneel and grab his prosthetic, easing it against my leg.

"What are you doing?"

"Giving you a massage…" I say casually, rolling his pant leg up and exposing the prosthesis. "You didn't specify *which* foot," I say, throwing similar words back at him.

"That's literally pointless. My right foot is rubber."

"And it'll get the best *rub* of its life," I muse, pulling off his shoe, then lathering lotion in my hands.

He watches me intently as I slowly knead my fingers around, making sure to even get the toes. His jaw ticks as I lick my bottom lip and stroke the base of his plastic foot. After five minutes, I wipe off the lotion, then help put on his shoe.

"How was that?" I ask with a smirk.

"Couldn't say."

"Guess it's my turn," I say, chuckling at his brooding expression.

We take a few more turns until I pick up a Sorry! card and send him back to start. This time, I'm fully prepared to get what I want.

"Whatcha got this time?" He arches a brow.

I stand between his legs, then straddle his lap with each of my thighs outside his. "You have to close your eyes and not move."

"Piper," he warns in his smooth baritone that sends shivers down my spine. His hands grip my hips as my body rocks against his.

"And no talking," I add.

His expression hardens, but he doesn't argue as he relaxes and does what I say. I lick my lips, determined to go through with this because if I don't, I'll always wonder *what if*.

I grip his shoulder with one hand and his face with my other as I lean in and brush my mouth over his. He sucks in a breath as I slide my tongue between his lips and add more pressure.

Without warning, he growls and squeezes my hips hard. The indentation of his fingers will most likely leave marks on my skin.

But I definitely don't mind.

"Now kiss me back," I whisper against his mouth, knowing he'll use that as an excuse if I don't *order* him.

"You're testing me, Piper. We shouldn't be this close," he murmurs.

"Why? I can feel how much you like it when I'm on top of you," I say, grinding down on his cock that's pressing against the fabric of my leggings.

"A million reasons. I work for your family. I'm much older. I'm supposed to be protecting you, not letting you get off on my dick."

A moan escapes me as I continue my rhythm, my clit begging for more.

"I could easily come just like this," I taunt, brushing my lips against his ear as he stiffens.

My breathing escalates, and so does his. Regardless of why we shouldn't be doing this, our bodies move together in perfect harmony.

Tristan groans, pressing into me. "You have to stop that, or I'll—"

A knock rattles on the front door before it cracks open. Before I can climb off his lap, Tristan throws me across the couch. I bang my head on the armrest and whimper at the instant loss of him.

"Hello, it's just me," Easton calls out. "I brought the goods!"

"Fuck." I hear Tristan mutter as he adjusts his erection, trying to hide how hard he is.

Easton enters carrying a paper bag and stops when he spots me lying awkwardly on the sofa. I didn't bother moving or adjusting myself since I was in complete shock that Tristan nearly tossed me to another planet.

He gives me a look, noticing how flushed I am, then I finally sit up and flash him a smile.

"I didn't know you were coming today," I say, trying to hide the unpleasant tone in my voice.

"Yeah, I know, but I got my shift covered so I could stop by a day early."

"Maybe a warning text next time. I nearly grabbed my gun," Tristan says.

He removed his holster before sitting on the couch, but it's still within arm's reach. We both know that's not what he was thinking about the moment Easton entered.

"Sorry, man." Tristan walks to the kitchen, then looks over his shoulder at me while he sets the bag down. "I have more groceries in the car."

Once he leaves, I take the opportunity to clean up the board game. Tristan and I stay silent as we wait for Easton to return. Once everything's on the counter, I help unload it.

"I brought you a surprise," Easton says with a grin.

"Me? What is it?" I ask, excited.

He digs in the last bag and pulls out a royal blue two-piece. "Brought you one of the shop's hottest summer items. Figured you'd need a real swimsuit in case Mr. Grouchy loosens the reins, and you wanna go jump some waves or catch some rays."

My jaw drops as I eye the gorgeous fabric. "You have no idea how much I want to kiss you right now!"

He hands it over, and I give him a hug. "I was just begging him earlier to let me go take a quick dip."

"It's not safe," Tristan blurts out, scowling and staring at how close Easton and I are.

"Well regardless, I'm wearing it. Whether it's around the house or on the beach." I smirk.

"So, what's for dinner?" Easton asks, breaking the awkward tension filtering through the air.

"Well, since you brought ground beef, I'll make some cheeseburgers and fries," Tristan responds, keeping his back to me as he shoves food in the fridge.

"I'm gonna go try this on. I'll be back in a bit," I say, grabbing my phone and giving them privacy. As confident as I felt earlier about climbing onto his lap, I am embarrassed about it now. I may be inexperienced, but I know he feels the same. Otherwise, he wouldn't have responded the way he did. The moment I touched him, his cock swelled, and there's no denying he liked it.

I might get burned in the end, but at least I can say I wasn't scared to put my heart on the line.

If only he'd take a risk with me and give in to what we both crave.

CHAPTER TWELVE

TRISTAN

DAY 16

THE DAY after Easton brought us groceries, he called and tore me a new one. Then I bitched him out for bringing Piper a swimsuit when I'd strictly told him not to. She's been begging to go to the beach for the past three days.

Apparently, he saw us through the window before walking in, and I know things would've escalated had he not come. He lectured me—not about crossing the lines—because he's concerned that *she'll* be the one hurt in the end. Inevitably, Piper will take a piece of me with her when our time is over. Not to mention, if her father finds out, he could blackball me from being a bodyguard for anyone else.

Surprisingly, Piper hasn't mentioned what happened between us, and I fully expected her to. By how she avoided eye contact during dinner, I could tell she wasn't happy. By the next morning, she was back to her usual self.

My phantom pain has been intense today, so I've tried to stay busy and walk around to manage it. The only time it's not bothering me is when Piper and I hang out. Listening to her talk about her childhood and lifestyle, what she enjoys about filming, and other random stuff keeps my mind off it long enough to ignore it. Now I crave being around her, not just to ease the pain but also because she intrigues me.

For the past three days, I haven't stopped thinking about the way she devoured my lips while boldly grinding against my cock. My only regret is not kissing her back.

It's both a blessing and a curse.

My brain can't make up its mind because my body wants every inch of her.

I know the risks and still...I struggle with setting boundaries.

"Can we please go to the beach today?" She sticks out her bottom lip, folding her hands and pleading. "It's the Fourth of July. You can't deny me on a holiday."

I arch a brow, trying to hold my stance while she looks up at me with sweet, innocent eyes.

"It's risky," I remind her.

"Life is full of risks," she retorts with a grin. "I could slip walking up the stairs, smack my head, bleed out, and die. So keeping me inside doesn't stop me from getting hurt."

"Jesus, you're morbid."

"And considering my clumsy ass, it's actually possible."

I sigh, pinching the bridge of my nose. "Alright, fine—"

"Ahhh! Yay! Oh my God, I'm so excited!" She rushes toward me, wrapping her arms around my waist.

"But there are rules," I tell her, pulling her back.

She rolls her eyes. "Of course."

"You stay within five feet of me at all times. I'm bringing my gun, and if I tell you it's time to go, your ass books it without argument. Got it?"

She gives me a salute. "Yes, sir."

I shake my head at her sassiness but secretly enjoy it.

"I'm gonna change! Make us some sandwiches!" she calls out and rushes to her room.

I nod, hoping I haven't made a horrible mistake.

"Oh my God…I'm in heaven," Piper moans as she lies on a beach towel, soaking up the sun that's beaming on us.

Since it's a private beach, most people are residents of the area or locals boating on the water. But regardless, I'm constantly checking our surroundings.

"Would you mind putting sunscreen on my back? I wanna flip over but don't wanna burn."

I swallow hard at the thought of touching her. By the glimmer in her eyes, she knows damn well what she's doing by asking.

But as usual, I struggle telling her no.

"Sure." I grab the bottle as she rolls over.

"Can you untie it for me first?"

I stifle a groan. "Yeah."

Leaning over, I unknot the strings, then brush my fingers over her soft skin. She rests her cheek on her forearms and closes her eyes, giving me full access to her body. I rub the lotion in my palms, then start at her shoulders and work my way down.

"Oh my God, your hands feel amazing," she whimpers. "It's been too long since I've gotten a massage."

"You get them often?"

"Usually once a week."

"Wow, so you're going through withdrawals," I tease.

"Shut up." She smirks. "I usually have knots in my neck and shoulders from being on my laptop so much. The hot stones are my favorite."

"Want me to find some seashells and scrape them over you?" I mock teasingly, rubbing her lower back.

"You're so rude!" She bellows out a laugh, slightly sitting up so she can smack me. As she does, her bikini top falls and reveals her bare breasts.

She catches me staring but doesn't hurry to cover herself. Instead, she watches for a reaction, but I don't give her one.

"Do you want your legs done too?" I ask instead.

"Sure." She lies flat, and I re-tie her top before continuing.

I dig my fingers into her thighs, brushing the bottoms of her ass cheeks as I massage the sunscreen in. Her breath hitches as I slide a hand between her thighs, and she spreads them so I can get the inside of her leg.

Slowly, I move down to her ankles, taking much longer than needed, but I can't stop. Touching her like this, seemingly innocently, is anything but. Piper's made it clear she wants to cross the line, and I'd be lying if I said I could resist her for much longer.

"If you weren't stuck here with me, what would you normally do for the Fourth of July?" I ask as I press my fingers into the pad of her foot.

"Probably go to a huge party at the Hamptons. Boating, drinking, the usual twenty-one-year-old shit," she states.

"Would you film it?"

"Some of it, like packing my bag and picking out my clothes for the week, maybe a swimsuit haul, then probably the drive there with a few friends. Stuff that'd bore you, I'm sure."

I chuckle. "Most likely."

Just another reminder of our age gap and how different our lives are.

"It probably wouldn't be as fun as it'd look, though. I don't really have close friends. It'd be all for publicity and photos."

"How come?"

"I don't trust anyone long enough to let them in because I've been screwed over and taken advantage of too much. Learned that the hard way when I was in high school. Then as I got older and grew my platform, girls used me to climb the social ladder. They'd tell me what I want to hear, then turn against me."

My brows raise, anger fueling my blood as I think about the assholes who did her dirty. "Wow, I'm sorry to hear that. I had no idea it was that bad for you."

"Believe it or not, I find it hard to fit in. I'm either too much or not enough. Having you around the past six months has helped me not feel so alone, even if you were paid to be with me."

The urge to pull her to my chest is so damn overwhelming, I almost do it. I ball my hands into fists to stop myself.

"You don't need people like that in your life. From what I've seen during the past couple of weeks, they'd be foolish not to want you as their friend."

"You're just saying that. I know you think I'm materialistic and shallow."

"Materialistic, yes. I never thought you were shallow."

"Superficial?"

"No."

"Tell me what your real opinion of me is," she challenges.

"And no sugarcoating it. I'll know if you're lying." She points a finger at me with a serious expression, and I hold back my laughter at her attempt to be authoritative.

"I think you're gorgeous, smart, funny. Parts of your career make you act like somebody you aren't, but I get why you do it. You're playing the part your subscribers expect so they'll keep watching."

"I can't decide if I should be insulted by that or not."

"The *real* you...that's what counts. Who you are for social media, that's who you allow them to see. But you've shown me a deeper side, and I like being around that person, not the Piper Montgomery persona."

"My whole generation grew up being online, constantly checking how many likes or subscribers we have, reading comments, and using that as a metric to validate our self-worth. It's a hard habit to break," she states with a hint of sadness in her voice. "It's a vicious cycle of wanting to be liked and seeming valuable."

"You don't need outside validation, Piper. You're more than enough without it. I might not be into social media and oversharing, but I can understand why you do. Validation from strangers will not make you a better or happier person."

"You're right. I thrive on it, and it's one of my fatal flaws. It's why I was so devastated about not being able to check or read what was being said about me. Regardless, it shouldn't matter because this is my life, and I should be allowed to take a break without everyone thinking the worst of me."

"Absolutely. The people you're seeking validation from are always the first ones to throw you under the bus," I add.

"Ouch, it hurts when you say it like that." She blows out a breath as she contemplates my words. "I can't wait to get online and tell them to mind their own damn business."

I chuckle when she laughs, loving the way it sounds from her mouth.

"So, returning to our earlier convo, what about you? Dare I ask about any of your Fourth of July traditions?"

I slide my hands up her legs, not wanting to break contact but knowing I've covered every inch of her skin with sunscreen. After I set down the bottle, I move back to my towel.

"I'm not a huge fan. Let's just say that."

She furrows her brows as she looks over at me.

"Of traditions or just this particular holiday?"

"Fireworks," I state. "It's triggering. The first year I heard them after returning home, I had a panic attack. I try to avoid them if I can."

"Oh my God, Tristan. I didn't even think about that. I'm such an insensitive ass." She sits up, adjusting her top. "We don't have to stay."

I shrug. "It doesn't matter. I'll hear them from in the house too, considering how close they'll be."

Piper frowns. "You can borrow my AirPods. They're noise canceling, so they should help drown out the sound."

Leaning over, I cover her hand with mine. "It's okay. I've gotten better at tuning them out."

"We can leave before they start," she reassures me. "And I'll find something to distract you so you won't even think about it."

I grin, appreciating her concern and thought, but it's too late. I hear gunshots in my sleep.

"Can we go in the water?" Piper asks thirty minutes later once her skin has baked. "I need to cool down."

"I can't submerge my prosthetic, but I'll stand on the shore."

"You can't ever get it wet?"

"It's water-resistant, like if it's raining or water splashes on it, but it's not designed to be submerged. It can damage and rust the various components. I'd have to wear a special prosthetic if I wanted to swim with one on."

"So you'd have to take it off if you wanted to go in a pool or something."

"Yes. But I'm not doing that out here. It'd make me too vulnerable in the event something happened to you."

She pats my thigh. "Don't worry, nothing's gonna happen. My stalker would've already come for me by now because I'm just too irresistible."

"Don't make jokes like that," I warn.

She sighs with an eye roll, climbing to her feet. "C'mon. I'm going in, so you better come play lifeguard."

I quickly follow and watch her from where I stand on the sand. She teases me every chance she gets by diving in, then standing up and showing off her gorgeous curves.

After fifteen minutes, she finally comes out, water dripping down her chest and legs.

"Have fun out there?" I muse, reaching down to grab her a towel.

"I did, but it would've been more fun had you joined me. Maybe someday you'll get a fancy water prosthesis and swim with me."

I chuckle at her verbiage. "Don't hold your breath."

"Oh, come on. You gotta loosen up a little. You're more tense than the day your brother almost caught us fooling around."

And there it is.

When I meet her eyes, there's a mischievous flicker behind them.

"Surprised it took you this long to bring it up," I say honestly, sitting on my towel while she lies down on the hot sand instead of laying hers out.

"Honestly, I was hoping you would say something. I can't be the only one trying to move this relationship forward."

My eyes widen at her choice of words, and I nearly choke on my tongue when she finally bursts out laughing.

"Your face, oh my God. If you weren't already sitting, I'd bet my life there was a stick stuck up your ass."

"You tempt and tease me in ways I've never experienced before," I admit. "It's been a battle, and I'm struggling with how to deal with it."

Piper stares intently at me as if she wasn't expecting the truth. "Then maybe it's time to stop fighting the inevitable."

"I wish it were that easy, Piper. A lot of variables are at play. I can't be impulsive and not expect to pay the consequences."

"Are you saying I'm impulsive?"

"Most twenty-one-year-olds are," I confirm. "I don't fault you for it. I just have a lot on the line if something goes bad."

She shrugs casually. "Perhaps you should try it then. Randomly doing things because it seems like a good idea can lead to some great times."

I don't respond because my mouth would end up between her legs if I did. I'm already hanging by a thin thread that's on the verge of snapping, so I keep my mouth shut.

The sound of the waves crashing is so relaxing that Piper's eyes grow heavy. When she falls asleep, I keep my gaze on our surroundings. I don't like the disadvantages of being in such an open space if Jack did show up, but I know how badly she needed this today.

"The fireworks are gonna start soon. Do you wanna head

in?" she asks when the sky turns red and yellow.

I meet her eyes. "Sure, if that's what you want."

"I'm fully baked and might be shaking sand out of every crevice of my body for a week."

"In that case, maybe you should use the outdoor shower before going in so you don't get it all over the house."

"Fine with me." She grabs her stuff as I pick up the cooler and my gun.

Once we're at the house, we set our things on the patio table, then head to the stall.

"The water's gonna be cold," I warn her before opening the door. "I'll grab you a clean towel."

"Wait…you're gonna leave me here by myself?"

Fuck. I can't do that. Other than the porch light shining above us, it's nearly pitch black out here.

"No, of course not. Guess you'll have to dry off inside." I shrug. "Let me know when you're done and—"

"There's room for two," she says, moving under the stream. "The cool water actually feels nice on my skin."

I step in and allow the door to shut behind me. "You sure you aren't crowded with me here?"

"Well, you do take up a lot of space." She chuckles, licking her lips as her gaze studies my chest. "But I like it. Makes me feel safe."

I nod, reassuring her I'm not going anywhere. Piper leans slightly to one side, giving me access to the water, and I quickly rinse the sand off my shoes.

Without warning, Piper removes her bikini top and bottoms, letting them fall on the ground.

"What're you doing?"

"I had sand in my suit," she says innocently. "It was itching my skin."

As soon as she spins around and bares herself to me, I fight every urge to touch and kiss her. This isn't the only time she's been naked in front of me, but it's the first I've allowed myself to fully look.

"Like what you see?" she playfully asks.

"Inappropriately so," I admit.

"When are you going to stop fighting this attraction between us?" She slides her hands down her hair, squeezing out the excess water.

"Until I can no longer control myself around you," I grit out, wondering if that time is now.

"I've tried everything to make you break, but you're stubborn as hell. You know how many times I've had to get myself off since you won't?"

My jaw clenches at the reminder of hearing her only a few nights ago. Piper moaning and panting as she fingered herself to an orgasm is something I'll never fucking forget.

An orgasm I wanted to taste.

"Show me," I blurt out.

Her eyes snap to mine as a blush covers her cheeks. Then she lowers them down to my shorts and notices my cock bulging against the fabric. She arches a taunting eyebrow, then slides a hand between her thighs and swipes a finger through her lips.

I grind my teeth, keeping my hands to myself while contemplating swatting hers away so I can take control.

"I've been wondering if someone like you would be able to get me off…" she says, playing with her clit as she brushes two fingers over it. "I'm an expert at self-pleasure, but you're all business and hardheaded. Surely, you won't know how to do it."

I nearly choke out a laugh, gripping the top of the wooden

shower stall. My fists are ready to punch a hole in them if she doesn't stop torturing me. "You're hilarious."

She shrugs, her breath hitching as she increases her pace. "Prove it then."

"You don't want to push me, Piper. I'm not gentle and am seconds away from taking what we both want. Put your swimsuit on and get inside the house."

Piper sticks out her delicate tongue, slowly licking the edges of her mouth as her eyes roll back. Her hand moves faster, and by her heavy breathing, I can tell she's close to coming all over herself.

"Watch me," she demands. "Watch what you do to me."

My gaze involuntarily lowers as I try to talk myself into leaving, but my feet stay planted.

She screams out in pleasure, her legs shaking as she rubs her clit faster, and when she nearly slips on the water, I catch her with one arm.

"Oh my God…" she mutters wildly before bringing two fingers to her mouth. Then she sucks on them with a deep groan.

And just like that, the thread fucking snaps.

Gripping the hair at the back of her head, I pull her toward me and capture her lips. She gasps at the sudden movement, but I keep her stable as I cage her against the wall.

"I want to taste your come," I murmur, lowering my hand between her legs and scooping up her juices. Then I bring my fingers to my mouth and suck hard on them. "Fuck. You're so sweet."

"You like it?" she asks.

"Goddammit, Piper." I bring our foreheads together, my cock screaming to be released and consumed by her. "One taste and I'm already fucking addicted."

CHAPTER THIRTEEN

PIPER

THE MOMENT TRISTAN'S mouth and hands are on me, every part of my body screams *finally*. I knew he'd cave once he accepted our feelings were mutual. Understanding Tristan on a deeper level solidified my attraction to him. I know he's hesitant, but exploring the chemistry between us is more than worth the consequences.

And Tristan's willing to risk it all too.

"Goddammit, Piper. One taste and I'm already fucking addicted."

His words are music to my soul, but I need more.

I turn off the water. "Please don't just tell me what I want to hear. Only touch me if that's what *you* want."

"Look at me," he demands, and I do. "You should know I'd never feed you bullshit. Every word I've said has been one-hundred-percent genuine. Never doubt that."

I nod, appreciating his openness.

"Trust me, I wish I were strong enough to resist you, but trying to stay away is exhausting. I can't fight it anymore."

My heart pounds while the blood rushes to my ears, and my stomach fills with butterflies. "Thank God."

Tristan cups my face, then crashes his mouth to mine. His tongue explores mine and steals my breath all at the same time.

"You're shivering," he murmurs. "We should go in."

I frown, but he's right. The fireworks will start any minute.

"Okay." I push open the door, but Tristan quickly closes it.

"You're naked." He lowers his gaze to my breasts. "You can't go out like that."

"No one can see us from here."

"Take my shirt." He pulls it over his head, and I lick my lips at the sight of his chest and abs. "Stop staring and put it on."

I chuckle at his arrogant tone and do what he says. It falls to my knees. "I'm keeping this, by the way."

The corner of his lips tilts up slightly. "Ready?"

When I nod, Tristan takes my hand, then leads me to the house. He puts on his holster and grabs our stuff off the table, then opens the door. After he's locked the door behind us, he unloads everything. I tell him I'm going to warm up in the bath.

"Wish you could join me…" I taunt, walking backward toward the stairs.

"I'll be waiting for you right here." He flashes me a wink that makes my clit throb.

"Or you could come and watch like the bodyguard you're supposed to be? I promise to provide you with a *much* better show than the fireworks."

His wide grin tells me all I need to know, and within seconds, he's following me upstairs.

Once I'm in the bathroom, I turn on the water and add

some of the bath salts Easton brought. Tristan stands with his arms crossed, staring at me as I undress. His cock bulges in his shorts, and I wonder what it'd take for him to let me suck him off. I've given head a few times but have never really liked it. However, I think I'd *more* than enjoy having him in my mouth.

"What are you thinking about?" he blurts out.

"Huh? What makes you think I'm thinking about something?"

"You have that look on your face," he tells me. "You're lost in thought."

I smirk as I dip my toes into the tub, then slowly submerge myself.

"Just reliving the moment you finally touched me and wondering if you'll ever do it again." I slide in deeper, letting the water glide over my breasts.

"That was a moment of weakness," Tristan states defensively as I catch his eyes lingering on my chest. "I shouldn't have done that."

Without responding, I spread my thighs and dip my hand between them. My body's still buzzing from earlier, and I'm getting worked up all over again.

"Then tell me how I should touch myself," I say, rubbing circles over my clit. "Because now that you've helped me orgasm, I'd like another."

I look over and see his jaw tense.

"You know exactly how to do it," he growls. "My dick's hard just remembering your taste."

My heart pounds faster as I rub harder. "Show me how you touch yourself," I demand. "I want to watch."

Instead of arguing, he leans against the counter and slips a hand into his shorts. Once he lowers them, my mouth waters just thinking about feeling him between my lips.

"God, you're so thick." I seductively stare at him stroking his length.

"Thrust a finger inside your cunt," he demands, and the hoarseness of his voice heats me to the core.

I push a digit between my legs and arch my back as I seek out my pleasure.

"You're tight, aren't you, baby?"

"Very," I admit, loving how he says that. I press the palm of my hand against my clit and add more pressure.

"Add another one," he commands. "Fill yourself full."

Tristan grips his dick firmer as the vein in his neck threatens to burst. He's getting off on watching me, and I'm about to explode from the way he's looking at me.

"Tristan, I'm so close," I murmur, pushing my palm harder as water splashes around me.

"Don't come. You wait until I tell you."

"I-I..." My entire body spasms as my release shoots up my spine and down again to my legs. I suck in my bottom lip as I suppress a moan, my breasts rising and falling as I try to gain control. "Oh my God."

"You finished without me."

"I couldn't help it," I pant.

Tristan walks closer, palming his cock and taunting me with every thick inch. "Now you need to help me."

I adjust myself, scooting closer to the edge of the tub, and reach for him.

"Open your mouth."

Looking up at him through my lashes, I do as he says and stick out my tongue. Moments later, he slides himself between my lips, and I quickly realize he's much bigger than I thought.

"Breathe through your nose, sweetheart." He grips my hair at the back of my head, tilting it up and guiding himself down my throat. "There you go. Take all of it, my sassy girl."

I narrow my eyes at him as I coat his length, then cup his balls. He hisses between his teeth, and I can tell he's close.

"Fuck, Piper. You're way too good at this."

I stroke him with my other hand as I glide my tongue around his tip. His hips slightly buck, and I can tell he's sensitive there.

"Oh, shit." He yanks away until I release him, then pumps himself until he spills on my breasts. "Goddamn."

I rub his come over my nipple before sucking it off my finger. Tristan watches me with lustful eyes as he tucks himself into his shorts.

"Is this where you admit you've had another moment of weakness?" I throw back the words I knew he'd live to regret.

His gaze hardens. "No. I didn't touch you this time."

"But you let me touch you."

"I did." He smirks.

"So, what's the problem? We're both adults, consenting to giving and receiving pleasure."

"The only problem I see is you're in there instead of my bed."

After rinsing off the soap and getting out of the tub, I wrapped a towel around my body. Once I dried off, Tristan led me to his room as nervousness soared through me.

"Are you okay?" He studies me as he sits on the bed and pulls me to stand between his legs.

"Yes, but I think I'm in shock," I answer honestly. "I've wanted you to kiss and touch me for so damn long."

Tristan cups my face with both hands before pressing his lips to mine. "I'll never do anything you don't want. Don't be afraid to communicate with me. That's the only way I'll understand your needs and limits."

"Then I guess it's a good time to tell you I don't really know what my limits are...I haven't experienced what I like or don't like yet."

If he's surprised by this confession, his expression doesn't give it away. A part of me thought he knew, but it's not exactly something you randomly blurt out.

"I look forward to finding out what they are then," he says. "Just know I'll never hurt you and will keep you safe in and out of the bedroom."

I chew on my bottom lip, loving the sound of that. "And what do you like? What are your preferences?"

"Well..." He slides his thumb slowly over my bottom lip. "When I tell you to sit on my face so I can lick every inch of your pussy, I mean for you to suffocate me. Don't hover. Literally *sit on my face*."

My eyes widen in shock. The few men who have ever gone down on me were always between my legs, never underneath me. But Tristan seems more experienced and ready to please me the right way.

"Remember when you asked me how I have sex?"

A blush creeps up my neck and face. "Vividly, yes."

"I like to give pleasure before receiving it, which means once you've come on my fingers and face, then I'll take off my prosthesis."

"So you *do* take it off?"

He smirks. "Usually, yes. It's not super comfortable to wear in various positions. It can also weigh me down."

"Interesting." I grin.

"Lift your arms," he commands.

As soon as I do, the towel drops to my feet. Tristan's gaze lowers between my thighs, then he slides a finger down my slit.

"How are you so goddamn wet already?"

With just one touch, my breath hitches. "Because I've been thinking about you being my first for months."

"You sure you want that?"

"Does my arousal not give it away?"

"I'll need to taste you to be certain," he taunts, licking his finger.

Tristan backs up on the bed and lays in the middle, then motions for me to follow.

"You were serious about me smothering you?"

"Trust me, sweetheart. When I need air, I'll find a way. The only thing you need to worry about is giving me complete and total access to your pussy."

I crawl up his body, then straddle his head as I hold the headboard. I've never been in this position before, and I can't help feeling self-conscious that my most intimate part is directly in his face.

Tristan grips my waist, then smacks my ass. "Sit."

Relaxing my hips, I lower myself until his tongue is against my clit. I blow out an intense breath, rocking against his facial hair. He grips my ass cheeks and spreads them apart as he drives his tongue deeper.

"Holy shit," I pant out, hardly able to speak as he masterfully teases my clit. I've never felt anything like this, and the sensation is almost too much.

After a couple of minutes, Tristan pushes me up slightly as he flicks and sucks my pussy lips.

"Jesus. I think my legs are going numb."

He lifts me a tad higher. "Then you're almost there."

Before I can respond, he pulls me down, adding more pressure, and rubs circles over my throbbing nub.

My fingers squeeze the headboard as a wave of pleasure shoots through me. The air gets caught in my throat as the eruption takes over, and Tristan's moaning vibrates through me.

Before I know what hits me, I'm shoved off the ledge without warning. It's nothing like I've ever experienced before. Getting one orgasm from a guy was rare, but *two*…this man is an anomaly.

Tristan taps my thigh, and I take that as my sign to move off him before I kill him with my vagina.

"Please tell me I didn't do that wrong." I lie on my side next to him.

Tristan looks at me, then dramatically wipes my come off his beard. "You were fucking made to sit on my face, baby. You wanna taste?" He arches a brow, waiting for my approval.

"I wanna taste you," I retort.

"That's not my rule."

There were rules?

"*Your* pleasure is my priority," he reiterates when I flash him a confused look.

"And I came…twice," I remind him.

The corner of his lips swipes up into an arrogant smirk. "It's adorable you think *twice* is a lot."

"It's not?"

"No, baby. Not with me at least. I want your legs trembling. Your throat raw from screaming my name. And my handprint bruised into your ass. Once I've pulled every orgasm from your body, then I'll let you touch me."

"You're going to make me beg for it, aren't you? As if I haven't seen you stare at my tits and ass for the past two weeks."

He chuckles with amusement, rolling over and capturing my mouth. "What can I say? They're pleasant to look at, even when you're scolding me about my cooking."

Tristan palms my breast and pinches the nipple. I yelp with surprise.

"I've jerked off to the image of your tits bouncing in my face. I came so damn hard and unexpectedly, I couldn't reach for a towel fast enough and ended up making a mess all over myself."

I bite on my lower lip, picturing that very thing and how hot it'd be to witness. "I wanna see that."

Without waiting for his answer, I slide his shorts down and allow his cock to spring free. The tip is wet. He's just as worked up as I am.

Next, I straddle his waist but don't sit yet, giving him just enough space to stroke himself.

"Except this time, instead of having to imagine it, you'll get the real show." I arch my back, making my breasts bounce.

"Jesus Christ, Piper...your juices are leaking all over me." He dips a finger between my legs, then places it in his mouth.

"I'm so wet. I could easily fuck you right here and now."

"We need to get you ready first." He grips his shaft, stroking himself a few times before he rubs it between my pussy lips.

I've been dreaming of the day I'd lose my V-card, and I honestly had no clue it'd be with Tristan, but now I can't imagine it ever being with anyone else.

"Tristan, I want you inside me," I beg, clinging to his shoulders as he pushes in slowly before sliding back out. "You're being a tease."

"I hate the thought of hurting you, Piper. The things I want to do to you have to be done with caution. I can't just pound into you when you're this tight."

My patience is thinning as he rubs the tip along my slit some more. I love watching the way he handles himself, tightly gripping his girth and roughly stroking the length.

"Are you going to let me devour you again first?" I ask, prolonging the moment we'll finally cross that line.

He nods, releasing his hold on me. I kneel in front of him as he repositions himself, giving me easy access to fully take him in my mouth.

"*Slow*, Piper. I'm not coming until I'm inside you. I have a condom in—"

"No. I'm on birth control. And I want to feel you inside me —raw and thick—with nothing between us."

"Fuck, baby. I can't wait to fill your tight little cunt full."

His words draw heat through my body as my willpower of waiting comes close to snapping. I take his shaft and feed him down my throat. His hips buck as I swirl my tongue around his tip, then suck as he thrusts harder.

"Goddamn, your smart mouth is vicious," he hisses. "You've gotta stop that."

But I don't.

I squeeze my palm tighter, hollow my cheeks, and move faster.

"Piper!" he scolds, and I stifle an amused laugh. "I said *slow*."

I ignore his request, dying to feel him lose control and taste his arousal. Before I can continue, though, Tristan sits up and fists my hair.

"Did you not hear me?" He tightens his grip, making me lose my rhythm.

"When have you ever known me to follow the rules?" I challenge.

He brings his other hand to my chest and twists my nipple. "And when have you ever known me to allow you to break them?"

I smirk. "I guess today's the day I find out."

"Piper, I'm trying to be gentle with you and not choke you with my dick, so don't push me on this."

"Is that what you've been fantasizing about? Is that what you like?"

"I like hearing you moan my name, whether you're sucking me off or I'm eating you out. Even the times you're touching yourself in bed."

"Then you better give me a *reason* to scream it."

CHAPTER FOURTEEN

TRISTAN

As soon as I tasted Piper's arousal on my finger in the shower, I was fucking doomed. I'd fought it for as long as I could, and once I crossed the line, I knew I wouldn't be able to deny her any longer. The push and pull was too strong, and I was weak against her.

Now she's kneeling in front of me, begging me to claim her how I've always dreamed, but I can't keep the thought of hurting her out of my head. This will be her first time, and as much as I want to pleasure her and take us to the next step, I know she'll be uncomfortable. It's why it's critical that she listens, but as usual, she's stubborn and defiant.

"Climb on top of me. You'll be able to control the pace and rhythm. I'll guide you through everything." I remove my shorts, revealing every inch of my prosthetic. I love that she's curious about it and hasn't been afraid to ask questions. Most people avoid it altogether as if it's not a part of me.

Piper wipes her mouth and straddles my lap as I drag her lips to mine. I intertwine my tongue with hers, feeling her relax as she rocks against me. She pours her soul into this kiss, and I give mine right back. I want this to be special for her, a moment she'll never forget—a moment *I'll* never forget—and most importantly, I want her to enjoy it.

My prosthetic is still on, but it'll work as long as we're in this position. As much as I'd love to bend her over and spread her ass cheeks, I won't until she's fully ready.

I lie back, giving her full access to my body. "Take my cock and fill your pussy, baby. Go at your own speed."

Piper takes me in her palm as she sits up slightly. She presses the tip against her clit, then slowly down her slit, covering me with her wetness. Every nerve in my body is on fire as I try to contain the willpower not to impale her with my dick. The teasing is torturous, but I know she needs to get used to me.

"How's that feel?" I ask her as she takes in just a couple of inches.

"Tight."

"You're telling me," I muse.

Without warning, Piper slams herself all the way down until she hits the bottom.

"Jesus Christ!" I shout at the same time she screams, "Holy shit!"

"Why did you do that?" I ask, worried she hurt herself.

"I'm not patient," she admits, lowering her eyes.

"Look at me, Piper," I demand, and she does. "Are you okay?"

"I think so."

"Are you in pain?"

"Yes, but it's bearable."

"Slide up and coat me a few times so you loosen up," I explain. She does as I say, the movement feeling so goddamn good.

Piper holds herself up on my chest, arching her back and barely rocking. I grip her hips, allowing her to take the reins while making sure she doesn't go too fast—at least until she's no longer uncomfortable.

"I think I'm getting used to the pressure," she says around a moan. "It's tight, but it doesn't hurt anymore."

Thank God.

Though she might be sore tomorrow.

"Go as fast or slow as you want," I say, massaging her breast as I flick the nipple.

"What feels better for you?" she asks.

"Everything you do will feel fucking amazing. Don't worry about that."

Piper's breaths are erratic as she rides me, and after a while, I thrust my hips into hers. "You're doing so good, sweetheart. You feel amazing." I blow out a harsh moan, trying to hold back my release as long as possible, but between her sucking me off and her tight pussy, I won't be able to avoid it much longer.

"Can I go faster? I think I can handle it."

"Do whatever you want." I lower a finger between her legs, rubbing circles over her clit. "You might not come from penetration your first time, so I'm going to help you get there."

"That's so sensitive," she breathes out. "Keep doing that."

I grin at her eagerness as she increases her speed. My balls tighten as she squeezes me even harder. I smack her ass with my other hand, earning a yelp in return.

"You have all the perfect qualities I'm obsessed with," I tell her, adding more pressure to her clit. "Your tits and ass were made for me."

"I hope my bubbly personality is included on that list," she mocks.

"That's what got us here in the first place," I tease, and she rolls her eyes.

"Well, it certainly wasn't because of *your* outgoing personality."

I slap her ass harder. "Quite confident for someone who's at my mercy."

"How so? I'm the one fucking *you*."

Christ, I'm going to hell for what I'm about to do, but nevertheless, I do it anyway.

I sit up, wrapping an arm around her waist, then maneuver her underneath me. My cock glides out as I move down her body and shove two fingers inside her pussy.

"I was just letting you *think* you held all the power."

"That was rude…now get back inside me." She pouts.

"Give me five seconds. Tease your clit for me," I demand, then sit up and start the process of removing my prosthesis. I glance over my shoulder and watch as she spreads her legs wide, revealing her pink pussy and slick juices.

I move my sleeve suspension down, take off the socket, then the liner, and socks. Once I'm done, my residual limb is bare. It's not nice to look at, covered with skin grafts and scars, but she's already seen it, so I'm not worried it'll freak her out. But I'm also not used to being this exposed around people. While my movements without my prosthesis can be unsteady at times, I don't let it limit how I pleasure her.

Once I'm ready, I crawl between her legs and take over, then dive inside her pussy and taste her arousal. Piper wraps her thighs over my shoulders, and I don't stop until she's coming on my tongue.

"Holy shit," I pant, moving up, then capturing her mouth. "I'm addicted to that."

"Fuck me," she demands, and I smirk at her urgency.

Gripping my shaft, I slowly ease inside, watching her reaction with every inch I thrust. Once I'm all the way in, she releases a sigh and lifts her hips.

"I can't get over how well we fit together," I whisper in her ear as she widens her thighs. "So goddamn good."

"It feels amazing. I never knew it could be this way," she admits, digging her nails into my back.

"I want your come all over my dick, baby. Think you can do that for me?"

She nods, unable to speak as I pound harder and faster, but I keep an eye out for any discomfort. When she tenses, I know she's close, so I sit up and lower a hand between us. As I massage her clit, I keep up my pace, and within minutes, she's moaning my name.

"That's my good girl. *Fuck*," I hiss as her pussy squeezes me so hard, I come without warning. "Shit...that was intense."

Once I've filled her, she collapses, and I tower over her, then kiss her.

"Was that enough reason to scream my name?"

"How are you still so arrogant even after you get laid?"

"It's my special skill." I wink, then press my lips to her forehead before climbing off. "Are you okay, though?"

"I feel like I ran a marathon but without any stretching or water. But it was amazing." She releases a contented sigh, and I chuckle at her analogy.

"Stay here, and I'll get a towel and some water."

I move down the bed, grabbing my prosthetic. She picks up the blanket that fell onto the floor and wraps it around herself as I get dressed. "Can I watch you put it on?"

"Sure."

She looks at my stump and furrows her eyes. "I never noticed how many scars you have. Makes you even more badass."

I snort. "Easton says I should've gotten a shark tattoo to make it look like it was bitten off."

"Oh my God, that's horrible!" She laughs.

I shrug. "Nah, he was just trying to be funny. I had thought about getting a tattoo but decided not to. The scars remind me of what I went through and how I shouldn't take life for granted. No tattoo could be more real than the marks that bomb left."

"You're a hero, Tristan."

"No. I'm not." I roll on the liner, then the sock before grabbing the socket. I move into a standing position, then place my leg in and pull up the sleeve. Once it's secured, I face her and press my mouth to hers. "Be right back," I say, slipping on some shorts.

After I use the bathroom, I go downstairs to grab a couple of bottles of water. Setting them on the counter, I wet a washcloth before getting a towel from the linen closet. As I walk upstairs, I think about my past and how easy it could be to open up to her. It's not something I talk about freely, but I feel comfortable enough to discuss it for the first time in years.

"Lie down," I tell her when I enter. "Spread your legs a little."

She watches me intently as I sit on the edge of the bed and press the warm cloth between her legs. "You'll most likely be sore for a bit."

"Is there blood?" she asks self-consciously.

"A little, but that's normal."

After she's clean, I dry her off and give her some water.

"That was the best way I've ever avoided fireworks," I taunt with amusement as I lie next to her and cover us up. I keep my prosthetic on just in case she needs anything else before she falls asleep.

"Yeah? Well good. Should we meet up every Fourth of July, keep the tradition going?"

"Independence Day sex? Sure, why not. Can I still bang your brains out the other days of the year, though?"

She shoves her elbow into my side, giggling, and I turn over toward her with a smile. "They remind me of the day of the explosion," I admit. "The noise is triggering because they sound like gunshots or bombs. I don't remember much from that day, only the explosions going off. I have dreams about it, but in them, everything's black. Just the noises are there."

"Were other soldiers there?" she asks.

"Yeah, there were eight of us. I was in the back of a Humvee with another guy, and we were the only ones who made it out alive."

"Oh my God, Tristan. I'm so sorry. Where is he now?"

"He overdosed shortly after we were released. The pain was too much."

"I'm so sad to hear that. How devastating."

"Very much. We spent months in a German hospital recovering and only had each other since our loved ones couldn't visit. My family could only talk to me over FaceTime, or we'd text when I wasn't in extreme agony. I was already in a bad place having to deal with this new normal, and then a week after we flew home, I heard of his passing. It wrecked me pretty hard."

"Did you have any idea he was struggling?"

"No, but I should've seen the signs. I was too into my own survivor's guilt and pain to notice."

She places her hand on my cheek and kisses me.

"His passing knocked some sense into me. I refused to give up on life just because it had gotten hard. I was an emotional mess, which was the first thing I got help for. After I was medically discharged, I found a few bodyguard positions. I couldn't take my second chance, one my brothers didn't have, and waste it. I was determined to make the most of my life."

"You had a great outlook. I'm sure many wouldn't have."

"You're right. Most can't get the help they need, and that's something that has to change."

"I never knew that about you, Tristan. It really changes my perspective. Guess I always interpreted how serious you are about your job and keeping others safe as arrogance, but it's more than that."

"*Especially* when it comes to you. I wanted to put a bullet in Jack's head the moment I saw him."

"Then you'd be in prison," she counters. "And I'd hate to have to visit you behind bars."

"That's better than me having to visit your gravesite."

"Geez, that turned morbid real quick." She glowers. "But maybe when Jack's finally caught, I can thank him for bringing you and me together."

"You better not," I growl, then lean over and swipe my tongue along her bottom lip. "We should get some sleep."

"You're right." She pulls off the covers, then shifts on the mattress.

"Where do you think you're going?" I reach for her wrist, halting her from leaving.

"Going to my room? I thought you wanted to go to bed."

"I do, but you're staying here with me."

As I say those words, I still can't believe this is where the day ended. Every moment with Piper seems surreal. A part of my brain screams never to let her go while the other reminds me of our age difference and how opposite we are. At this point, if her family disapproves, I don't know what will happen. Being together when she returns home isn't an option. I'll have no reason to stay in New York once her dad fires me for sleeping with his daughter.

But I'll steal every opportunity to be with her while we're here—even if it's temporary.

The next morning before we get out of bed, I kiss her senselessly until she begs for more. Knowing she'll be sore, I eat her out until she moans my name. Once she catches her breath, she offers to cook breakfast.

As we head downstairs, I get a call from the Montgomerys' private investigator. He explains there was a sighting of Jack in South Carolina. By the time the cops were called, he was gone again. Maybe allowing Piper to go to the beach yesterday wasn't the best idea, but it was good for her and made her happy. However, I would've never forgiven myself if Jack had happened to find her outside. He might not be in Florida, but at this point, it's too dangerous not to stay focused.

Once the call ends, I do a perimeter check, making sure everything's secure, but I'm more paranoid the closer he gets.

I decide not to tell Piper unless she asks.

"How's it going in here?" I ask once I return from my phone call.

"Well…I've thrown out two pieces of French toast, spilled a

cup of orange juice, and realized halfway through that the wrong burner was on."

"That's better than the smoke detector blaring." I chuckle. It's adorable she's trying, though.

"Don't place your bets yet. I still have to finish cooking." She glances over her shoulder and sighs. "No man will ever want to marry me if I can't even cook breakfast."

I snort, grabbing the spatula from her hand. "Let me teach you then."

Once a couple of pieces are ready, she refills our juice glasses, and we eat and talk. I ask how she's feeling, and she admits she's going to take a painkiller and a hot bath.

"Okay, I'll clean up here." I kiss the top of her head before she takes off.

I send a text to Easton with an updated list since he's supposed to come in a couple of days. Then I go look for Piper.

"Hey, have you seen my hairbrush?" she asks as she searches through the bathroom drawers.

"No. Where'd you have it last?"

"In here, where I always keep it." She begins opening and closing the cabinet doors.

"Did you look in your room?"

"Yeah, twice. And your room. Where the hell could it have gone?"

My paranoia goes to Jack.

"I'll add it to Easton's list so he can bring you a new one," I offer. "Unless you find it before then."

She sighs in defeat, frustrated. "Okay, thank you. I guess for now, I'll just let it go free and wild."

"Just like your personality." I wink.

CHAPTER FIFTEEN

PIPER

DAY 20

BEING AWAY from home and my sister is starting to gnaw at me, but I'm happy Tristan's here to distract me. We get to be alone without interruptions, and I've learned so much about the man who has quickly stolen my heart.

As I lounge on the couch, Tristan moves my legs and plops down under them. His firm hand rubs up my thigh, and he smiles. Seeing him like this, so relaxed and comfortable with me, makes my heart flutter.

"Easton won't be able to come today due to the bad weather moving in. He'll be here as soon as it passes."

I look out the windows, noticing the overcast sky outside. "What's going on?"

"Tropical storm."

My eyes widen, and I begin to freak out internally because I have no idea what that means, especially right here on the coast. "Oh my God, will we be okay staying here?"

He nods, but I quickly grab the remote and turn on the

weather channel. Meteorologists are on the scene as the wind causes the rain to fall sideways. In the background, the sky looks deadly as the waves crash.

"Looks like Tropical Storm Carolyn is coming in strong. The surface winds are measuring around sixty miles per hour, and they're expected to gust up to over seventy," the guy explains.

"Do you think it'll make landfall as a category one hurricane?" the woman in the studio asks just as the man's hat flies away.

"No, Bethany. But it's close. Floridians, if you're near the beach, stay indoors. Could see some flooding as well as downed trees and powerlines."

As they continue chatting, I feel like I'm having an anxiety attack. Tristan notices and scoots closer.

"Come here," he says, opening his arms. I crawl onto his lap, and he holds me tightly. "Don't worry."

"I've never been through anything like this before." I create enough space to meet his eyes.

He leans forward, brushing his lips across mine and tucking loose strands of hair behind my ear. "When Easton and I were younger, we'd go surfing during tropical storms."

I laugh. "Are you kidding me? Out in *that*?"

"The waves were much larger than normal, and being out in the ocean was dangerous because of the rip currents, but we were young and stupid, completely fearless. It was some of the best times. Growing up around this kind of weather desensitizes you to it."

"So, the roof isn't going to blow off? A palm tree isn't going to uproot and land on the house? Floodwaters aren't going to rise ten feet and get in the house?"

He chuckles. "No. Nothing like that. We'll probably get a

lot of rain for a couple of days and some strong winds. We might lose power."

"Thank goodness." I loop my leg around his waist and straddle him. "So I guess that means you'll have to keep me occupied?"

Tristan grips my hips as I grind into his cock. He groans out, and right now, I want him more than ever.

"Damn, sweetheart. I wish we could continue what you started, but we should probably do some preparation before Carolyn makes her arrival. Tempting, though, real fucking tempting."

Tristan glances at the TV. "We have about an hour before it makes landfall."

"Okay, fair enough." I reposition my body and let him stand.

Tristan goes to a storage closet in the hall and pulls out a few vintage-looking flashlights.

"I'm gonna look in the shed outside to see if there are more. Don't move," he says.

Five minutes later, he returns with a fancier lantern and a bottle of liquid.

"I don't think I've ever seen anything like this in my life," I tell him as I follow him to the breakfast bar.

"Experiencing lots of firsts these days." He winks.

"Thanks to you. It's been an eye-opening experience and has shown me a lot about myself."

"Yeah?"

"I just didn't realize how much life I've been missing until I broke out of the cycle, ya know? Not being online, not being around my parents, not having every luxury handed to me." I linger for a moment, thinking about everything we've gone through so far.

"So, being stuck here hasn't been so bad?"

"Only because of you." I waggle my brows. "Now, teach me how to light this lamp from the 1800s."

Tristan choke-laughs. "It's not *that* old, but we might need this."

"What's that?" I point at the bottle he's emptying into the bottom of the glass reservoir.

"It's kerosene. It burns for a while. This wick goes from the top down to this well and keeps the flame fed. You only have to worry when you run out of wicks, but we've got extras." He pulls them from his pocket.

"That's cool. Another thing to add to my list of things I've learned."

Tristan grabs some scissors from a kitchen drawer, then trims the wick before lighting it. He puts the glass cover over the top. "This knob will make your flame larger or smaller."

I reach forward and turn it, and when the room brightens up, I realize how dark it's gotten outside in just a short amount of time.

Once the counter is full of flashlights, extra batteries, and a lantern, he meets my eyes.

"Now we need to fill the tubs."

"Huh? Why?" I ask, following him.

"In case the power goes out, and we need to use the bathroom. The water well is powered by electricity. The water pressure won't be strong enough to flush if it's off. It'll only be a trickle otherwise."

My mouth falls open. "You're joking, right?"

"Do I look like a comedian?"

All I can do is laugh because a tropical storm coming while I'm here is just my luck.

"Let me show you how you'll do it." He grabs a small

bucket from the bottom of the pantry, then we go to the bathroom.

"So, you'll take the top off the back of the toilet." He lifts it and sets it to the side.

"That looks heavy."

He smiles. "Then you fill the bucket with water and pour it in here."

"And that works?"

Tristan chuckles. "Yep. Tropical storm flushing at its finest."

We make our way downstairs, and Tristan fills an empty milk jug with water, then places it in the freezer.

"What sorcery is this?"

"The frozen gallons will help keep items cold for longer if we lose power. Oh, and if that happens, we'll need to keep the fridge door closed so our food doesn't spoil."

I tuck my hair behind my ear. "We should've gotten a generator."

"That works fine until you run out of gas and can't drive to a station to get more. And eventually that will happen, trust me. I've lived through it."

Letting out a deep breath, I watch as the dark clouds and angry waves roll in. "I'm anxious."

Tristan moves close, wrapping his arms around me. I squeeze him tight, breathing in his manly scent. "If it gets too bad, your dad said he'd send a private jet to get us, but it's predicted to pass quickly."

I push away. "He did?"

"Yeah. Making sure you're okay is my number-one priority, Piper. If I thought it would be a dangerous situation, we would've already been on the road headed toward the airport. I won't let anything happen to you, ever. Do you trust me?"

A smile slides across my lips. "Absolutely."

"Okay then."

We sit on the couch, and he unmutes the TV.

"If I had to choose anyone to be with during this, it'd be you."

He chuckles. "That makes me happy, considering weeks ago, I'd probably have been your last choice."

I chew on my lip. "You would've followed me anyway. So it's not like I would've had the option to choose."

"You're damn right about that." Leaning over, he places his strong palm on my cheek and kisses me. My tongue twists with his, and I melt into him, wanting and needing more. His stomach growls, and so does mine. Eventually, we break away, both breathless and greedy for one another, but I also know we need to eat.

Tristan puts a pizza in the oven, and we devour the whole thing when it's done. Not too long afterward, the rain taps against the house. I guess I didn't realize how many damn windows there were until now. The palm trees bend and buck, and I hope the ocean doesn't rise any farther.

Lightning strikes nearby, and I nearly jump out of my skin. Tristan reaches over and firmly places his hand on my thigh.

Instead of continuing to watch the news, I grab the remote and turn off the TV. I close my eyes and count to ten. Sure, we've had storms in New York, but it's nothing like this.

"Hey," Tristan says, reaching for me when he notices I'm a ball of nerves. "Come here."

I go to him, and he holds me close. "You okay?"

"Not really," I admit, hating that I sound like a scared little girl.

"I know how I can take your mind off things." He waggles his brows.

"And how is that?" I smirk, eager to hear what he has to say.

All he does is arch his brow, and I read between the lines.

Standing up, I slide down my shorts and throw off my shirt, revealing my see-through black lingerie set I packed just in case.

"Damn," he hisses, studying my curves.

I give him a sexy striptease, humming T-Pain's "I'm N Luv" song. Tristan's eyes never leave my body.

"I think when I get home, I'm gonna get one of those stripper poles installed in my room. That way, I can give you a proper show."

He smirks. "I'd love to watch you practice."

Laughter escapes me as I pull my hair from my ponytail. It falls around my face, and Tristan swallows hard.

"You're so beautiful, Piper. I'm so damn lucky."

"No, I am," I counter, then spin around, touch my toes, and wiggle my ass in his face. He reaches forward and smacks it. The pain mixes with pleasure, and I'm ready for a repeat of yesterday.

"You're a filthy little girl," he hisses when I take my bra off and throw it at him.

When I straddle his lap, I feel his hard erection, and the friction as I rock my hips has my body begging for more of him.

"Those jeans need to come off right now," I demand, falling to my knees and reaching forward.

I unbutton and yank them down forcefully while taking his boxers too.

His thick cock is at full attention, and I admire every

bulging vein before tracing them with my tongue. As he runs my fingers through my hair with a groan, I'm encouraged to take him deeper into my throat.

"I can't wait to taste you," I admit, loving his eyes on me as he cups my breasts and pinches my nipples.

"I have a confession to make," Tristan grunts out.

"What's that?" I say, between sucking and licking.

"I watched you touch yourself upstairs after you drank all that old whiskey."

I lift a brow, thinking back to my moment of weakness when I wanted Tristan so bad it hurt. He constantly teased the fuck out of me, even if he was trying to avoid me.

"Yeah? Did you like what you saw?"

"I always love watching you play with your perfect pussy," he admits. "Seeing you pleasure yourself with my name on your lips was something I won't forget for the rest of my life. You're enough to bring any man to his knees."

I smirk. "Well, maybe I should start an Only Fans account when I get home. There are a lot of YouTube stars who make millions and get tons of free sex toys."

"Hell no," he growls as I stroke him. "I don't like to share, Piper."

"Oh, so I'm yours now?"

He nods. "Baby, you know you're mine. And as far as sex toys, I think my cock is enough, but if you want something else to play with, we can use whatever else you want."

"I like the sound of that." I slip my panties down my legs and step out of them. Straddling Tristan's lap, I carefully slide down on him. I suck in a breath as I take him all the way in.

"You're so fucking tight," he groans as his firm hands squeeze my waist. The pressure of his length and girth inside me is so intense, my pussy clenches as he stretches me wide.

Once I've adjusted to his size, I slowly glide up and down, then pick up the pace. Tristan snags one nipple between his teeth, then his strong hands move to my ass cheeks.

"Oh my God," I scream. "Harder, please," I beg, and Tristan slams deeper up into me.

"Yes, yes, just like that," I whisper. The sound of my skin slapping against his thighs bounces off the walls. His thumb finds my clit, and as soon as he adds pressure, the orgasm builds so quickly that I can barely control myself.

"Don't make me come yet," I tell him, wanting to be brought to the edge a few times first. I slow down, my pussy screaming and throbbing for release.

"So goddamn beautiful," Tristan murmurs, moving to my other nipple. I meet his mouth, greedily twisting my tongue with his, wanting to devour him.

Once I've caught my breath, I try to pick up the pace but find it harder to continue. I'm teetering, and as soon as I'm ready to spill over, I stop. We do this until I'm so close to coming I can barely breathe.

Tristan continues slamming into me, and I love that he's teasing himself too. He's brought me to the edge at least seven times, then slowed his pace. The next movement I make has every one of my muscles tightening, then contracting.

"Damn, girl. You ride me so good," Tristan grinds out as I bounce on his cock. The sensation of him sliding in and out becomes too much. My body unravels as an earth-shattering orgasm rocks through me.

Seconds later, he's gripping my hips and releasing inside me. I ride him until my body is ready to collapse. He wraps his strong arms around me as I fall forward and hug his neck. My pussy convulses, and I'm soaking wet.

"I've never met a girl who likes to be teased so much."

I know I should get up, but I don't think I'll be able to stand. "I want mind-blowing orgasms that rip through me, and edging is fun, like a game. How long until I give in to the pleasure?"

"I love that you enjoy it. It's sexy as fuck to feel how close you are and then stop. Just one touch and you'd explode, then when you do, your pussy nearly squeezes my dick off. Feels amazing."

I meet his eyes. "Thankfully, you've got the stamina to keep up in your old age."

Tristan grabs a handful of my ass. "Always, baby."

Once we've both come down from our high, we clean up. I lie on the couch naked, and he spoons me from behind, enveloping me in his arms as we watch TV. A satisfied smile splashes across my face, and I can't help but feel relaxed and sated. Tristan has a way of doing that to me. Nothing in the damn world could worry me right now, not even a tropical storm. Instead of being concerned about the rain, it makes my eyes heavy. Or maybe the mind-blowing sex is to blame. Either way, I know I'm safe—Tristan has already proven that much to me.

After we fall asleep, a text wakes me. I grab it from the kitchen counter, my legs already feeling sore, but I welcome the sensation.

I unlock my phone and plop down on the opposite end of the couch as he stays in place.

Kendall: Hey! Just checking on you and making sure everything's okay.

My face contorts.

Piper: Why wouldn't it be?

Kendall: Because Florida is getting pounded right now.

I'm tempted to respond that Florida wasn't the only thing getting pounded. Instead, I relax and chuckle.

Piper: Oh yeah, it's raining, and we've got some high-speed winds, but we should be fine. Tristan said most of it will blow over by tomorrow.

Kendall: Do you have power?

Piper: Right now we do, but that could change.

Kendall: Gah, I hope not for your sake. Being without power SUCKS! Trust me. But speaking of Tristan… how are things going so far? Were you able to put him under your magical Piper spell?

I hesitate for a moment, deciding if I should tell my sister the truth or keep it to myself for now. Knowing I won't be able to hide it from her for long anyway, I decide to go for it. She won't tell a soul, and all of my secrets are safe with her.

Piper: Well…

Kendall: ?????

Piper: If I'm being honest, I don't know how to start this conversation.

Kendall: Did you two bump uglies? Do the dirty? Is your cherry popped?

She inserts an eggplant emoji with the three water droplets, and I beam.

Piper: Yes!

Kendall: OMG! That means you're not a virgin anymore. Piper...this is HUGE.

Piper: I know! And trust me, huge is an understatement. Even crazier is how hard I'm falling for him.

Kendall: Sis. WHAT?

Piper: Ugh, yes. I've never had a serious relationship before, and it's all new to me, but I can't help it. This is way more than just a crush.

It makes me wonder if we could ever be more than what we are right now in this beach house. When we return to New York, it might all change.

Kendall: There's something magical about being isolated with someone. I mean, look at Ryan and me. Without that record blizzard, I'm convinced he would've never given me a chance based on his assumptions of me. We really got to know each other. So, who knows, maybe this is the beginning of something special?

Piper: I hope so. I know Mom and Dad wouldn't approve, but I can't deny what my heart feels.

Kendall: And what about Tristan? What does he say?

I let out a sigh.

Piper: He fought against it at first because of his reservations, but ultimately, he knew we had chemistry.

She immediately responds.

Kendall: Reservations about what?

Piper: Our age difference. How he's my bodyguard. My social status. I get it because the odds are stacked against us in the real world.

And unfortunately, I can't change any of it.

Kendall: Aw, don't say that. You have no idea what could happen. Next year, you could be getting married and having babies.

Her text makes me snort. Tristan glances at me and lifts a brow.

"I'm chatting with Kendall," I tell him, and he nods, knowing how often we joke around.

Piper: I'd love for us to get a real chance without all

the outside noise, but I'm not sure how realistic
that is.

**Kendall: If that's what you want, that's what I want
for you. Just please promise me one thing.**

Piper: What's that?

Kendall: Protect your heart at all costs.

I read her message a few times before finally replying.

Piper: I will.

The last thing I want is a broken heart. Setting down my
phone, I crawl over to Tristan and allow him to hold me.

"I think I have a sex hangover." I giggle, releasing a
contented sigh.

He laughs into the softness of my neck. "And just think,
I've only gotten started with you."

CHAPTER SIXTEEN

TRISTAN

DAY 22

THE RAIN and wind stopped yesterday afternoon, and the house suffered no damage. We didn't lose power either though we would've been prepared. I tried to keep Piper's mind off it the best I could, and I think I was successful. Being with her so intimately already has me thinking about the future, about us, and where we go from here. I never imagined someone like her would be attracted to me or that I'd have a chance in hell with her. How am I—a disabled veteran with a dark past—her type? I question that every single day, and she proves I'm what she wants every moment she can.

As I'm making a pot of coffee, Piper enters wearing the T-shirt I gave her when she fully gave me herself. I love seeing it hang to her knees, especially when she's not wearing anything under it. She wraps her arms around my waist and squeezes me while kissing my bare back. I turn around and press my lips to hers, noticing she has her brush in her hand.

"You found it?" I ask.

"It was under my bed." She snickers. "So the mystery is solved."

I give her a grin, somewhat relieved because for a moment, I thought maybe, just maybe, Jack had found us and stole it. He's said weird shit about her hair in emails.

"So, there's something I want to talk to you about," I say.

She blinks up at me with bright eyes. "What's up?"

"Easton's coming today since the roads are open, and he's already suspicious of us." I leave out the part where he bitched me out after seeing us fooling around on the couch.

"Okay. *And*?"

"I think it's best if we keep what's happening between us to ourselves and not make it obvious that we're…a thing. The last thing I need is for my brother to give me a hard time."

Her smile fades. "Why? Are you embarrassed by me?"

"No, no," I blurt out. "I swear it's not like that. I don't want the whole world to know about us until we figure out what we're doing and how we're going to navigate being together outside of our safe space."

She gives me a sarcastic grin. "Oh okay. Sure. Got it. Understand, *sir*."

"Piper…" I narrow my eyes at her typical attitude. I should've known she'd take it the wrong way.

"Nope, don't worry about it. He won't suspect a damn thing." She shrugs, then makes herself a cup as soon as it's done brewing. Without another word, she goes upstairs

I let out a frustrated breath, but I really can't do anything about it either. It's for the best, regardless of Piper's frustrations. Embarrassed isn't how I'd describe how I feel about her, but I also know my brother will hound me, and I don't want to second-guess my decision to be with her. My parents would know before he left the house, and no telling who else would find out. If the wrong person catches wind of it, the internet will be convinced the rumors are true. That's stress she doesn't need, and I'd feel guilty for being the cause of it.

Easton arrives an hour later. I help him carry the groceries inside, and when we return, Piper's dressed in tight jeans and a crop top. Her hair is pulled up, and she's put on bright red lipstick and mascara.

"Hey, Easton!" She moves toward him, holding out her arms for a hug. He gladly squeezes her, hanging on a little too long for my liking. While I'm tempted to say something, I keep my words to myself.

"Missed seeing you," she says sweetly as she pulls away.

He chuckles. "Oh *really*? Well, I'm here now."

God, he's insufferable when women flirt with him.

Piper unloads the bags and gets excited about everything she pulls out. If I didn't know better, I'd say her camera was set up somewhere because she's giving Easton her YouTube Piper persona. However, I see right through her act.

"You literally got all of my favorites," she gushes.

He shrugs. "I've learned my lesson with you."

Piper laughs right on cue. "Well if you ever need anything, you just let me know, and I'll make sure to repay you for your services. Speaking of, I've been thinking about that promo post for your shop. Maybe next time you can bring me something else that I can pose in? The bikini was amazing, but do you have any thong swimsuits? I could set up my camera and take some sexy angled ones."

Easton lifts a brow and looks her up and down. "Actually, I think I do. It'd look hot on you too."

"Oh yay! I could even write Belvedere on my stomach, right here." Piper lifts her shirt higher, showing even more skin, and my brother's eyes nearly bug out of his head at how much she's revealing.

I clear my throat. "These groceries won't put themselves away."

"You should stay for lunch," Piper offers, ignoring me. "That way, we can talk more about it."

"Yeah, sure. What're you making?"

"I'm not sure yet…" She looks around, and I know for a fact she can't cook shit. Her eyes meet Easton's. "Maybe you can help me decide? I'm not the greatest in the kitchen."

Easton looks at the different items on the counter. "What about chicken Caesar salads? Looks like we've got everything here."

"Perfect," she sing-songs.

I stand back, watching her laugh at every one of his jokes. She bumps her body against his as they cook together. She even has the audacity to wink at him.

While I know she's trying to make me jealous, it's working because my stupid brother is feeding into her bullshit. Though I understand why because Piper's charming. It's one of the reasons she has millions of followers and why she's under my skin day in and day out.

After they've tossed in the dressing, cut and added the chicken, and made three bowls, we sit at the table.

"Oh wow, the puzzle is almost done," Easton says as he takes a bite.

Piper speaks around a mouthful. "Yep, I'm determined to finish it before we leave."

"Do you know how much longer you'll have to stay?" Easton asks.

"Nope. The sooner, the better, though." She meets my eyes, and there's a fire behind them.

Easton chuckles. "Yeah, I'm sure all of this has been a big change for you compared to what you're used to."

"A wake-up call is more like it," she asserts. "But I'll have *a lot* to post about when I'm released. Your shop being one of them."

His brow pops up. "Can't wait. This could be huge for us."

I swear he's flirting with her just to mess with me, not because he's actually interested. Regardless, it pisses me off all the same. Throughout the entire meal, I keep quiet, letting them continue their ridiculous charade. When I finish eating, I put my bowl in the sink, then go to the living room.

They continue talking, and eventually, Piper starts cleaning the kitchen.

"Well, thanks for inviting me for lunch. That was amazing," he tells Piper.

She smiles wide. "Yeah, it was! It was great chatting with you. We'll have to do it again sometime before I leave."

He leans down and gives her a side hug. "I'd like that."

I force myself to hold back a groan at their sudden friendship.

Easton comes over to me. "You good?"

"Fine," I say.

"If you need anything else, just text me," he tells me, then flashes a knowing smirk.

The bastard.

"Will do. Thanks for restocking us."

"Pleasure's all mine." He waves at Piper before leaving.

Once I hear his car back out of the driveway, she moves into the living room with her hands on her hips and stares at me.

"What?" I ask.

"I can't believe you treated your brother like that. You were so rude."

I scoff with shock. "Are you kidding me? What the fuck was that, Piper? You basically riled him up and left him with blue balls."

She gives me an innocent look. "I did *exactly* what you instructed."

"No, you went too far," I tell her.

"You told me to make it obvious nothing was going on between us, so that's what I did. Now you're pissed?"

I shake my head because she knows exactly what she did. "You're being immature."

That angers her more than anything else I've said. "Oh really? Now *I'm* the immature one. Sounds a bit hypocritical to me, considering you sat there and stewed in your anger while we ate."

"I wasn't stewing. I was letting you do your thing, practicing your bubbly YouTube personality on Easton."

She rolls her eyes. "So, I wonder what makes you more jealous. The fact that he was eating it up and flirting right back or that we're closer in age and you didn't like seeing us get along?"

I bark out a sarcastic laugh. "If you want my brother, go for it, Piper. I'm not stopping you. You're a grown-ass woman who does whatever she wants. But damn, you sure know how to make a man feel used. Guess being tossed to the side like a broken secondhand toy was bound to happen eventually."

"Are you fucking kidding me? I'm *done*. I'm done with you and this whole stupid conversation."

She storms off, but there was truth in what I said about feeling used. The way she could so easily be all over someone else like we never existed angered me. And if I'm being honest, it's one of my biggest fears when it comes to a woman like Piper. My heart beats rapidly at the way we blew up at each other. I hate that she walked away mad, but maybe space is what we need right now. We're both hurt and confused.

Hours pass and she still hasn't come downstairs. It's nearly dinnertime, so I whip up something quick. When she smells food cooking, Piper makes her way into the kitchen.

I serve up some steak and black beans, and we don't say more than a few words to each other while we eat. Once we're done, I clean up and decide to finally say something.

"So, we're not going to talk about what happened earlier?" I ask.

"I don't have anything else to say," she says from the living room.

I wipe my hands on a dish towel, then make my way to her until I'm close enough to pull her into my arms. "Piper, I'm sorry. I'm sorry for letting my emotions get the best of me and taking it out on you. I hate how I reacted."

She meets my eyes. "I don't think you're a broken secondhand toy, Tristan. I have no intentions of tossing you out. That was so hurtful to hear you say."

I nod. "You're right. I have a lot of insecurities and other issues I'm still working through. I don't know why I immediately get defensive and self-sabotage when something good in my life is happening, but it's a bad habit I'm trying to break."

"Well just know that you don't ever have to feel insecure with me. I don't always know what you're thinking. I'm typically really good at reading people, but it's different with you. You have a hard exterior and a wall around your heart, which sometimes makes it hard to understand your true feelings. But I want to knock them down and hope you'll let me be the one to do that."

I suck in a deep breath, relief washing over me as she gives me reassurance. "I think some see my hardness and ability to shut off the world as a strength, but I also know it's one of my weaknesses. Especially in the relationship department."

"Just be honest with me, Tristan. That's all I want."

I nod. "I don't know how to process what we're doing. It's been a long time since I've been in a relationship or fallen for someone so hard and fast. The truth is, there's something about my past I haven't told you."

She sits at the bar and pats the stool next to her. "Tell me, please."

I take a seat and swallow hard. "I was engaged to a woman named Willow."

Her eyes widen in shock just like I suspected. "When?"

"Before I went overseas. We planned on getting married when I returned home, but after hearing of the explosion and my injury, she called off the wedding and left me. I haven't spoken to her since."

"Wait, what?" Piper shouts, her face reddening. "Please tell me you're kidding."

I shrug. The pain she caused no longer bothers me, but the damage of what she did still affects me. "Nope. I woke up two weeks after the explosion since they put me in a medical coma due to the numerous surgeries. I tried to call her as soon as I could and learned she blocked me. Easton told me she had packed her things and moved out of our house."

"She didn't even tell you herself?"

"No. Pretty sure her heart was too cold to care."

"What a fucking bitch!" Piper says. "You risk your life to

fight for our country, and just because you lost part of your leg, she leaves you? What a heartless cunt."

I laugh at her choice of words but agree wholeheartedly. "Willow was a narcissist who only thought of herself, and it took being away from her for me to see that. I'm actually thankful she left before I returned. I thought I loved her, but once the blinders were off, I realized it wasn't a forever kind of love. She just did me a favor."

"That's why you're jaded about relationships, isn't it?"

I nod. "It's the root of my insecurities, yes. At the time, I was devastated and extremely angry. I thought if my fiancée couldn't even love me after I became an amputee, there was no way anyone else ever could. I was a broken man, inside and out."

"You know that's not true, right? You have your reservations because you're afraid to get hurt again, but you have so much to offer. More than she ever deserved. It was a thousand percent her loss."

"You have no idea what that means to me, Piper. I haven't allowed myself to get close to anyone since then, except you. I let you in as much as I could, but each day, you dug yourself in a bit more, and soon, you were in so deep, I knew I was in trouble." I chuckle, brushing my fingers along her cheek and wrapping a strand of hair behind her ear. "I don't know what we are or how our relationship will change once we're back in the real world, but it scares me to think of losing you. And those feelings brought my insecurities to the surface again. I found myself asking what a young, beautiful woman like you would want with an older man like me. I can't offer you the things you deserve, but I can give you my whole heart…if you want it. As long as you promise not to break it."

Her wide smile is contagious.

"I'm falling for you so fast and hard, I don't care what people say or think, and although I can't predict what's going to happen, I know I want to see where this goes. We deserve a real chance at being together because I can't imagine not being with you at this point. I want this. You. *Us*."

I lean forward, brushing my thumb across her soft cheek as I study her beautiful face. Slowly and passionately, I kiss her, pouring all of my emotions into it.

"I want that too," I confirm.

"I told my sister how I felt about you. She totally supported it and was happy for us," she admits when we pull away.

"Wow. You did?" I'm not sure why this shocks me, but it does. Honestly, I imagined Piper would want to keep me a secret because of who I am and how little I really have to offer a star like her. But then again, I keep going back to what she said earlier, when she first started to open up to me—money can't buy love or happiness. Deep in my heart, I know I can give her both.

"Yeah, I told her a few days ago. I think that's why it hurt so badly when you wanted to hide our relationship from Easton. Because while I know the odds are stacked against us, I want to openly explore this with you. But let me be very clear about one thing so you don't have any doubts. I don't give two shits what anyone thinks about us being together—my parents, my sister, my subscribers, or the media. At the end of the day, I'm in control of my future, and I can't let others dictate it."

Her words drive through my heart like a knife, and I feel like a huge asshole for wanting to keep her a secret. It's something I never should've done. I wasn't ready to have that conversation with Easton, but now I will as soon as I can.

"You mean so much to me, Piper. Words can't even describe how much you've already changed me for the better," I admit, noticing the sweet way she's looking at me. "I'm all in, babe. Right now and when we leave Florida. No more hiding or worrying about things we can't control."

Her smile grows wider. "I can't guarantee this whole thing will be easy."

"Nothing worth it in life ever is."

CHAPTER SEVENTEEN

PIPER

DAY 23

I HAVEN'T BEEN able to wipe the cheesy grin off my face since Tristan and I confessed our true feelings last night. Especially after learning about his ex-fiancée and how hard it was for him to give relationships another chance. Whoever that Willow chick is will be kicking herself as soon as we're plastered all over Page Six. Not that I care about making her jealous, but a little gloating never hurt. After hearing he was all in, butterflies settled into my stomach and have rooted themselves there. Every time he kisses me, they flutter as my heart beats harder. I've never felt this way before or been this happy in years. Our safe bubble is making me want to never go home.

Though we have insecurities about what the future holds, I've decided not to dwell on it until I'm forced. He knows where I stand and that we're in this together.

That's all that matters to me.

"I had the dirtiest dream about you," he murmurs in my ear as he spoons me under the covers.

"Are you sure it wasn't real? Especially after what we did last night," I tease, arching my back and wiggling my body against his erection.

"Hell yes, we did. In my fantasy, you were riding me reverse cowgirl style with your long blond hair flowing down your back, and your perfect ass was in my face. Then I woke up with the biggest wood." He slides his fingers around my body and squeezes my breast as his lips suck on my neck.

"I think we can make that happen," I say, then moan when he pinches my nipple.

"Good, because I can't get enough of you. I want to mark every inch of your body with my mouth and handprints, let every man in the world know you're taken. And *mine*."

"I don't think you'll have anything to worry about. The second I'm back in the public eye, they'll know." I smile at the thought of holding his hand and walking down the sidewalk as paparazzi bombard us with questions.

"Damn straight." He lowers his hand between my legs and growls. "My needy girl, always wet and ready for me."

"You do that to me. I always want you," I hum out as he rubs my clit.

Several minutes pass as he plays with my pussy, building me up and getting me close before he stops, leaving me in agony. I love the way he knows my body so well and how to please me, even when I didn't know what I liked. Tristan gives me exactly what I need while making me feel safe and secure in and out of the bedroom.

"Climb on top of me, baby. Display that ass for me." He gives me a smack before I straddle his legs and grip his shaft. Normally, I'd feel shy about having my intimate parts in any man's face, but Tristan worships me like a goddess. He feeds me compliments and reassures me he loves everything he sees. The way he praises in bed will never get old, and honestly, I get off on it now. I crave it.

"Tell me if I'm not doing it right, okay?" I say, worried I'll be unsteady in this position.

"Sweetheart, everything you do is perfect."

I playfully roll my eyes. Of course he'd say that.

Lifting up on my knees, I press the tip of his cock to my pussy and spread my wetness around him.

"You're such a sweet little tease," he groans, squeezing my waist.

Before we lose our minds, I slide down his length, each inch filling me up and making me whole.

"Lean forward and grab my ankle, then spread your cheeks. I'll get even deeper."

I smile in amusement at the way he says *ankle*. His residual limb is something I've quickly become accustomed to, and it doesn't bother me in the least, but there's always that fear in the back of my mind that I could hurt it.

"You laughing at me?" he asks playfully.

"Of course not." I glance over my shoulder, watching how he admires every inch of me.

"It's okay to laugh, my love. Wait until we go shoe shopping, and I have to ask the associate for two different shoe sizes because my prosthetic foot is a bit smaller. Their expressions are always priceless."

I chuckle, rocking my hips faster. "I bet you have too much fun shocking people."

Before he can answer, I squeeze his cock and fuck him harder, finding a steady rhythm. The sensation is almost too strong as he lifts his hips and thrusts upward. He's so deep, I can barely catch my breath.

"Yes, baby. You feel so good," he whispers before smacking his palm against my ass. I love the way he marks my skin. The mix of pleasure and pain turns me on even more.

His finger slides between my cheeks, and I anticipate what he'll do next. I relax and spread my legs wider.

"Jesus Christ, Piper. You're so goddamn sexy."

I hear his mouth pop as he sucks around his thumb before sliding the tip into my tight hole. I scream out in pleasure, loving how full it makes me feel.

"More," I beg.

He squeezes one ass cheek while pushing in deeper, and it's almost enough to push me off the edge.

"I'm so close," I tell him, nearly gasping for air.

"Fuck my cock, baby. You're doing so good riding me like this."

Moments later, my calves tighten, my toes curl, and a burst of pleasure seizes through me. Throwing my head back, I moan out his name. Tristan gives me the full reigns and lets me slow down as I ride the high.

"I can feel your come sliding all over, baby. Fuck, that was hot."

"So intense…" I sigh. "This position is dangerous."

He chuckles, wrapping a hand in my hair and pulling slightly. "Now you know why I woke up with a hard-on."

"You want me to stay like this, or should I turn around?" I ask, knowing he hasn't come yet.

"Baby, I'm ready to explode."

I take that as my cue to keep going. Straightening my spine, I bounce on his cock until he's gripping my hair so tight, I nearly explode again. The way he roars out his release sends a burst of satisfaction through me, knowing I'm the reason for it.

Once we've recuperated, I collapse next to him and wrap an arm over his chest.

"You're going to spoil me, waking me up like this each day," he says, cupping my face and pressing a kiss to my mouth.

"Just wait until I tell my father you're moving into my apartment. Then we'll get to wake up next to each other every single day."

He blinks at me.

"Shit, was that…too much? Too fast?" I mentally slap myself for my word vomit. "We should've talked about it before I just assumed. I'm sorry. Ignore what I just said."

"*Piper.*"

I look at him, swallowing hard.

"If you want me to move in with you, I'll pack the second we're back. I want to be with you wherever you are. You should know that by now." He smirks. "I didn't put up with your attitude for months just because I was on the payroll."

"You make it sound like you were a paid stalker."

Tristan smirks, plucking my bottom lip with his thumb. "I was."

Once we're clean and dressed, we head downstairs and make a quick breakfast.

"What do you think will happen if they never find him?" I

ask as we eat our avocado toast. I finally got Easton to bring the avocados I'd been craving.

"Guess that means you'll be stuck with me forever." He flashes a wink. This social media break and getting to spend time with Tristan has been the best thing that's ever happened to me.

"Well, if that's the case, can we at least move our hideout to Maui or Puerto Rico or something? My hair needs a break from this humidity."

"Then I'm afraid you're gonna wanna go north." He snickers. "Alaska?"

"I'll literally freeze to death. See, this is why New York is a good compromise. Gets all four seasons. I could easily bundle up in the winter or stay inside, and also have A/C in the summer." I take a bite of my toast and crunch loudly.

"Not everyone has central air in New York. It's a luxury," he says, and I laugh because he's right. "Jack will eventually run out of money and places to hide," he states. "Your parents are gonna want you back soon I'm sure."

"Or they're secretly enjoying me being away. They've never really supported me being on YouTube and sharing so much with the world. I think they'd prefer I lived like a nun."

"I think most parents want what's best for their kids, and for them, it's keeping you safe at all cost," Tristan tells me in his deep baritone.

We finish eating, then I offer to clean up while he showers. Before he goes upstairs, he pins his body to mine.

"Put your hands flat on the wall," he whispers in my ear as he presses his chest to my back.

I grin, then follow his orders, raising my arms and placing my palms on the wall.

"Good girl. Now spread your legs for me." His fingers

slide beneath my panties, then he finds my clit. "Fuck, you're wet again. You needy girl."

My breathing goes shallow as he flicks it faster. "Mmm…" I moan in response, arching my back to push harder against him.

Tristan works me up until I'm nearly screaming and begging him to give me what I want, but each time I'm close, he slows down or stops.

"Tristan…" I plead, rocking my hips. "I'm going to finish myself off if you don't."

"Tsk-tsk, sassy girl. You keep those arms up."

"Then quit teasing me," I hiss between clenched teeth. It doesn't matter that we just had sex an hour ago. I already want his cock inside me again.

He removes his hand. When I glance over my shoulder, I see him licking his fingers. "No touching yourself until I return. I want to watch."

"What?" I spin around with a scowl. "Don't leave me hanging. That's cruel."

He presses his lips to mine. "I like you riled up and begging for me. It'll be worth the wait, I promise. I'll be back in less than twenty minutes." He flashes a wink, and tingles zap through me.

The asshole knew I was teetering on the edge.

I narrow my eyes at him as he walks backward toward the staircase.

"Just remember, payback's a bitch," I say.

He chuckles with amusement, then heads to the bathroom.

I clear the table and put the dirty dishes in the sink. Instead of waiting for them to soak, I scrub them to keep my mind busy while I wait for Tristan. The man owes me one hell of an orgasm.

My mind wanders again to our conversation last night and how things have changed so fast. I don't want to lose him when we return to the city, and though I'm worried about how my parents will react, I'm not letting him go without a fight. People won't understand how we could possibly have anything in common because of our age gap and class differences, but that's none of their damn business. As long as we're happy, that's all that matters. I know my sister supports me no matter what and will have my back if needed.

Hands cover my eyes from behind me, and I gasp.

"Oh my God, I didn't even hear you come down," I tell Tristan. I was so lost in my head and tuned everything out. "You gonna finish what you started?"

He presses his body into mine and brings his mouth to my ear. I wait for his filthy words that I love so much, but they don't come. Instead, his tongue slides along my outer ear, and it's then that I feel something's off.

I try to turn around, but he doesn't release me. "Tristan?"

As I peel his hands off my face, I'm shoved harder into the counter as he grips my hips. When I look over my shoulder, my heart stops as I realize it's not Tristan. Beady dark eyes stare into mine, and it's the first time I've been this close to my stalker.

"Let me go," I demand, pushing against Jack, but he traps me in with his large body.

Before he responds, I open my mouth to scream, but he quickly covers it. I flail my arms, trying to get him off me, but he's too strong. After twisting my arms roughly behind my back, he slams me into the countertop.

"Jack, don't do this. Let me go," I plead behind his palm.

He grinds his erection into my lower back, and I fight the

urge to throw up. The way he's caging me in sends a shooting pain down my spine.

"Please, you're hurting me," I say as loud as I can.

Tristan's still in the shower and probably can't hear me from upstairs, but even if he could, he'd need time to put on his prosthesis, get dressed, and grab his guns. I can't help but wonder how the hell Jack found me or how he plotted to break in the moment Tristan wasn't glued to my side.

Regardless, I try to scream for him.

"Tristan! Help!"

"Shut the fuck up," Jack growls, then I feel pressure in the middle of my back. It's cold and hard like the barrel of a gun. "Make another sound, and I'll end you."

He roughly shoves a fist into my hair, then yanks my head back.

"What do you want with me?" I ask as he tightens his grip.

"You pathetic little slut, as if you don't know," he hisses against my ear. His hot breath feels like poison on my skin. "I *loved* you. We were made for each other. I only wanted to show you how perfect we'd be together and how much I'd cherish and touch you, but then you left. I was the good guy, and you ran from me."

"I don't even know you," I remind him. "You sent me threats and made me fear for my life. That makes you the *bad* guy."

"I was trying to stand above the other men attempting to gain your attention. I wanted you to notice me. If you'd given me a chance, I would've worshipped the ground you walked on and took care of you."

Bile rises up my throat, but I swallow it down.

"Look at me," he orders, keeping his tight hold on me.

I turn around, hoping I'll be able to escape, but then he

forces himself on me. My back presses against the counter as his arms cage me in. For the first time, I get a good look at him. He's not much older than me, but he's tall and muscular. His eyes are dark and hard. There's an evil man behind them, and I know he's here to harm me.

"The longer I had to search for you, the angrier you made me. Right now, I'm eager to cut your throat and watch the life leave your eyes. God, what a beautiful sight that'd be to have your rich blood all over my skin."

"You're obsessed with a person you only think you know," I tell him with venom in my tone. "You don't know who I really am."

Jack takes a knife from the sink and angles it at my throat. My heart beats rapidly as I try to steady my breath. He's getting off on my fear, and I refuse to give him that pleasure. As soon as I open my mouth, he stops me.

"Scream, and you're dead," he tells me. "Don't think I won't do it. I've been hunting you way too fucking long and am too committed now. I'm determined to see this to the end."

I swallow hard as the blade pushes into my skin. "You're going to do what I say and follow me out of here. Got it?"

Before I can tell him to go to hell, Tristan enters in a pair of jeans with his gun aimed at Jack. His hair and chest are still soaked from the shower. I blow out a small breath of relief, but it's quickly replaced with fear as I worry about Tristan.

"You have three seconds to beg for mercy before I put a bullet in your head."

Jack increases the knife's pressure while aiming his pistol at Tristan. Everything happens so fast, I can hardly process what transpires. An ear-piercing shot rings out, and I realize Jack pulled the trigger. Tristan immediately loses his balance and falls to the ground. I scream, trying to escape Jack's hold so I can rush over to him, but he yanks my hair so hard, it feels like he's ripping strands from my scalp. Jack chuckles, finding amusement in what he did as he drags me toward the door with him.

"Tristan!" I scream as Jack forces me outside.

I claw at his arm, trying to kick him off me, but it's useless. The adrenaline has me fighting for my life, but no matter what I do, Jack's unaffected.

"Please, just let me go. Tristan needs help," I plead as he walks us toward the ocean. The fear is so overpowering, tears surface and pour down my face.

"Stay quiet, or I'll go back in there and shoot his other knee," he warns.

I manage to connect my foot with the back of his leg, making him stumble.

"Wrong move, bitch." He tackles me to the ground face-first. Jack straddles my legs, yanking both my arms behind my back, then cuffs them.

"Please," I beg between tears. "Don't do this."

"Shhh…it's gonna be okay," he whispers while petting my head. "We're finally going to be together."

Oh hell no.

I need to get back to Tristan. He could be bleeding out…or worse.

Jack gets me on my feet, then leads me toward a boat anchored in the water. I frantically shake my head. "I'm not getting on that."

By some miracle, I break free of his grip, and even though my arms are restrained, I run toward the house.

"Nice try, you dirty cunt." He rams into me, making me fall again, then shoves his gun against my skull. "Try me again and see what happens."

"You're fucking crazy," I seethe.

He bellows out a laugh, lifting me up and leading me back to the water. "You haven't seen crazy yet."

Fear and panic nearly blind me as I suck in air.

"C'mon, get on." He leads me into the water, then shoves me on board, making it rock back and forth. This doesn't seem safe.

"Where are you taking me? We won't make it far," I warn as if I know anything about boats. But if one thing is certain, the ocean waves will overpower us. They're too large.

He starts the motor, laughing maniacally as he keeps his weapon pointed at me. I try to wiggle my wrists free, but it's no use. The cuffs are too tight. I need to stall him as long as possible so he doesn't take this boat any farther into the water.

"Jack, please," I plead calmly. "We'll die if you go any farther. The tide is in."

The boat roars to life, and he turns toward me with an evil grin. "At least we'll die together then."

"Help! Please, help!" I scream, praying someone hears me in the distance.

"Shut the fuck up!" he shouts, then whacks me in the face with the gun.

I yelp out in pain as I fall to my side. Fuck, that's gonna bruise.

"We aren't going far. Just to the marina. Think you can stay quiet for ten minutes, or do I need to stuff my dick in your mouth?"

My heart thumps as he lifts me up by my elbow, sitting me upright.

"Don't fucking touch me." I jerk my arm from his grip.

"Your wicked mouth is only making me harder, you ugly cunt. So if you keep opening it, I'm gonna use it."

I grind my teeth, not willing to test him on his threat. However, I won't think twice about biting it off.

Jack revs the engine again. I frantically look around, hoping someone is close enough to see or hear me, but most people are too far out on the water.

The rough waves make it hard to stay steady, and Jack curses as he struggles. Just as the boat turns away from the house and rocks with movement, a gunshot rings out. I scream, lowering my body as Jack messes with the controls, increasing the engine's speed.

I can't tell where the shot came from, but then there's another, and this time, it hits Jack in the arm. He suddenly jerks the wheel, and the boat rocks to one side, then the other. Large waves crash against us, flooding the boat. I shift to both sides, unable to steady myself because I can't use my hands. Jack loses control, and before I know it, the boat is tipping over.

As I fall into the cold water, I struggle to kick my feet since I can't move my arms with the handcuffs on. I can't bring myself up to the surface and start to panic.

I'm going to drown.

I'm going to die before I have the chance to tell Tristan I love him.

I hope he knows, but we never exchanged those three words. They were on the tip of my tongue, and now I regret not saying them.

If I somehow survive this, I won't think twice about it.

The cold and exhaustion take over as I grow weaker and am unable to fight to stay afloat. I look up and see the capsized boat drifting farther away as I struggle to breathe.

Tristan's the last person on my mind when everything goes black.

CHAPTER EIGHTEEN

TRISTAN

As soon as the boat capsizes, I run toward it and wait for Piper to swim up so I can help her out. I keep my gun aimed toward the water in case Jack reappears. I know the bullet hit him, but I'm not sure where. The boat was swaying hard, and I didn't want to risk him getting away, so I took the shot.

"Piper!" I yell, hoping she'll hear my voice and find me.

I struggle with what to do since my prosthetic can't be submerged, and there's a risk of it weighing me down. Not to mention I've been shot.

The bullet pierced the socket of my prosthetic. I immediately went down, the pain burning through me as I realized that stupid fuck had somehow hit skin. However, the socket acted as a shield, and once I realized what happened, I stood and bounced my foot to re-secure the seal and release the extra air. With the pressure of the prosthesis against my knee, the bleeding stopped, but it won't stay secure for long. The wound will need to be taken care of as soon as possible, but my only focus is finding Piper.

I'll need my backup liner once I get the injury looked at.

After a minute of waiting for her to resurface, I know something's wrong.

"Fuck it." I toss the gun and tear off my shirt before rushing into the cold water. "Piper!"

The pain radiates through me, but I push through it. I've been through worse, and I'll get through this too.

I dive in with long strokes, squinting my eyes to see. My mind goes back to when Piper told me she barely swims, and then my fear doubles.

Where the hell are you? Swim, Piper, swim!

I feel the movements of the waves as I try to push through them. She could be anywhere with the way they're violently slamming. Needing to go under where the boat tipped, I force myself down, then finally see blond hair. I kick my legs as fast as I can until I reach her, and that's when I realize her hands are cuffed behind her back.

Motherfucker.

I had no idea the asshole bounded her wrists since I could only see her upper half when I took the shot. Figuring he'd go down as soon as he got hit and that Piper could swim to me, I didn't think twice about it.

Now I could be the reason she doesn't survive.

Wrapping my arm around her waist, I hold her and use all my arm strength to get us to the surface. I have special training in water and can hold my breath for a long time, but there's no way Piper is capable. She's been down here too long.

I swim faster than ever before, sucking in air as I drag her onto the beach. Piper's unconscious, and the weight of my leg and soaked jeans cause me to trip and stumble on the sand. Pain shoots through my body, and I hold back a curse as I analyze Piper's condition.

"Baby, I'm here," I tell her though I doubt she can hear me. I quickly check her pulse and feel a weak beat.

I position her properly, tilting back her head, then perform mouth-to-mouth.

"Come on, Piper. Breathe."

I repeat the process, then start chest compressions. Then I do it again.

"Please, sweetheart. Fight for me."

After another minute of CPR, she finally coughs up water. I quickly roll her to her side so she gets everything out.

"Thank God." I cup her face.

She blinks up at me, tears welling in her eyes, then I pull her into my chest. "You're okay. You're okay, baby."

"Tristan? Oh my God, you're alive! I thought he shot you, and I lost you forever."

"He did, but I'm okay. I'll be alright. We need to get you to the hospital."

"I tried to stay above water, but I couldn't. He cuffed me," she explains.

"I didn't know until I found you. I'm so sorry."

"Wait, you went into the water? What about your prosthetic?"

"Yeah, I'm gonna need some new parts, but I'll be okay."

"Did you see Jack come out?" she asks.

"No. I didn't see him in the water either, but that doesn't mean anything."

"I saw the bullet hit his arm. Then he lost control of the boat, and it capsized against the waves. What if he was able to swim farther down and made it to another beach?" she asks with fear in her voice.

"Then we'll find him, baby. Don't worry. I'm not letting

you out of my sight again." I press my lips to hers. "I'm so sorry."

"This isn't your fault, Tristan. There's no way you could've predicted this."

"That's not how everyone else will see it. You were taken on my watch."

"My father's private investigators should've done their job and tracked him here. It was a failure on their part," she tries to reassure me, but the guilt of what happened is eating at me.

How the hell did he find her and get inside the house without me hearing it? The man is fucking Houdini.

Sirens blare in the distance, pulling my attention away, and I thank God they arrived so fast.

Before I rushed out of the house, I dialed 911 and blurted out the address as soon as a dispatcher picked up. I explained I'd been shot and my girlfriend was kidnapped. They said they'd send assistance ASAP.

Chaotic commotion commences as EMTs find us on the beach.

"Examine her first," I demand as they wrap a blanket over me, then one over her. "She nearly drowned."

"Tristan, no. I'll be okay. Let them take you."

"Piper, it's not up for debate. You're my responsibility." I move my gaze to the man in front of us. "Please, take her to the nearest hospital. I'll follow in the car."

Another EMT approaches with a steel cutting tool and frees Piper from the handcuffs. She throws her arms around me and cries.

"You saved my life. I don't care what anyone else says. Got it?"

"You need to get checked out, baby. Please, go in the

ambulance, and I'll meet you there." I press my lips to hers one more time.

People who nearly drown can suffer from many injuries, and though Piper is talking and looks fine at the moment, something internally could have been affected. I'm not taking any chances.

The EMTs transfer her onto a stretcher, and I watch as they put an oxygen mask over her face and a blood pressure cuff around her arm. As soon as they load her onto the ambulance and the doors close, I carefully make my way to the house, wincing with each step.

Luckily, I have extra liners and socks, but I'm afraid to remove them. If it starts bleeding out, I won't be able to get my prosthetic back on to drive. So instead, I take a bag with me and pull out my stash of narcotic pain meds that I keep with me at all times. I haven't taken them in years, but I've found comfort in keeping them close in the event I'd ever need them.

Today's going to be that day.

As soon as I arrive at the hospital, I pop two pills, then call Easton.

"Hey, I'm in town at Memorial. I got shot."

"Jesus Christ, man. Are you okay? What happened?"

"Jack found her. I'll explain more later. Piper was taken by ambulance after she nearly drowned. She's okay, but I made her get looked at just in case." My brother knows what water can do to the lungs from surfing so much.

"Wait, how'd you get there?"

"I drove."

He chuckles in disbelief. "So you get shot and then drive yourself to the hospital? Why am I not even a little surprised?"

"Because you know I'm a stubborn ass."

"Are you gonna see a doctor at least?"

"Yes, but first I need to call the Montgomerys, then check on Piper. But just thought I'd let you know what's going on."

"Appreciate that. Text me with an update. I'll come if you need me to."

"Will do."

After we hang up, I ring Mr. Montgomery, but he doesn't answer. Next, I call Mrs. Montgomery, and she doesn't pick up either. Instead of waiting for either of them, I find the nurses' station and inform them of who I am.

"We've contacted her parents already. They're en route."

"Oh okay. What room is she in?"

"I'm sorry, but I can't allow you to see her," the nurse tells me with an apologetic expression. "Her parents have requested no visitors until they arrive."

"But I'm her bodyguard."

"I'm sorry, Mr. Belvedere. You'll have to wait to get permission from them."

"She's over eighteen!" I argue.

"I understand that, but you're not family." She shrugs and doesn't say anything else.

"Fine. I need someone to look at my wound, please. My prosthetic got hit with a bullet, and the socket is filling with blood."

Her eyes widen as she lowers her gaze. "You got shot?"

"Yes. I don't think it went through, but it burns." Hell, it feels like it's being crushed too.

She grabs the phone and calls out a code. Soon, another nurse comes with a wheelchair and brings me to an exam room. I explain my situation and the details of what happened. As I slip off my prosthetic, blood flows out.

"You're lucky. Looks like it just nicked you on the inside of your knee. No bullet hole."

I look down in shock as she cleans it up. "How the hell is that possible?"

I felt it hit my socket. I felt the pressure against my skin.

"You were in distress, which can magnify your injuries and pain," she offers when I explain what happened.

Blinking, I wonder if that's possible. PTSD can cause the brain to play tricks on you.

The only solution I have is maybe my phantom pains were triggered by the shot. It felt extreme but resulted in a less serious injury than I thought.

While I'm confused as hell, I'm also grateful it's not worse.

"I'll bring the doctor in to look before I wrap you up. He'll probably prescribe you some antibiotics and pain medication if you need it," she explains.

I use that time to text Easton.

Tristan: Nurse says I'll live, but I haven't been allowed to see Piper.

Easton: Why the hell not?

Tristan: Her parents said no visitors, and I'm not family, so now I have to wait until they fly in.

Easton: When will that be?

Tristan: Who knows. No one will tell me anything. I'll probably need you to pick me up, though, since I won't be able to wear my prosthesis out of here.

My residual limb will need to heal before I can put it back on. Thankfully, I'll still be able to use the socket until I can get a replacement. However, I hate using a wheelchair and feeling powerless, but it's a necessary evil being an amputee. My biggest fear is losing mobility and being stuck in a chair. Just the thought gives me intense anxiety.

Ten minutes later, the doctor introduces himself and says he wants an X-ray just to be sure. Since there are a lot of skin grafts and scars, he needs an inside view. I agree since I'll be waiting for the Montgomerys for a couple more hours anyway. Once the results come back, he confirms there's no internal damage. I'm wrapped up and discharged.

As soon as I'm wheeled back to the waiting area, I only think about getting to Piper.

CHAPTER NINETEEN

TRISTAN

I'VE IMPATIENTLY SAT in the waiting room for the past two hours, and I still haven't heard any updates about Piper, nor have I seen her parents. My mind is going wild with thoughts on how she must be feeling that I'm not there with her. I can't predict how her parents will react. I wish I could tell them what really happened before they hear a washed-down version from the staff.

After another thirty minutes, Piper's parents finally walk in, and I wheel myself to them.

"Mr. and Mrs. Montgomery. I'm relieved you made it."

Her parents' faces are stone cold, and they don't even offer me a hello as Mrs. Montgomery stares at my leg.

"You're in a wheelchair?" she asks in shock.

"Yes, but I'll recover quickly."

"You're an amputee." Mr. Montgomery analyzes my wound sock.

"I am, sir. I didn't disclose it to you when you hired me because it wasn't a setback you had to worry about."

"Apparently, it was," he spits out.

I don't want to argue with them, so I don't bother responding.

"Can you please let the nurses know I have permission to see Piper? She's been all alone and is probably waiting for me."

Mr. Montgomery glares at me with a huff. "Absolutely not."

His words feel like a punch to the gut, and my body stiffens. "Sir, with all due respect, I'd like to see her."

"Tristan, unfortunately, I can't allow that to happen. My daughter wouldn't be in this position if you had done the job you were hired to do. You'll be lucky I don't sue you for not disclosing critical medical information about your ability to protect her." He lowers his gaze again.

"I did everything I possibly could." I look back and forth between the two of them. Her mother's lips form a tight straight line, and she doesn't say a word.

"Clearly not enough," he barks. "I'll need the keys to the rental car. As of…" He looks at his watch, then back at me. "Right now, your services are no longer needed."

"Won't you at least let me explain what happened?" I have no idea what they've been told, but it couldn't possibly be the truth. "Jack had a—"

He holds up his hand. "I don't want to hear excuses. My daughter is in the fucking hospital because of your incompetence. Keys. *Now.*"

I dip my hand in my pocket, then hand them over. Adrenaline rushes through me as my face heats with anger and frustration.

"Don't worry about returning to New York either. It's actually best if you don't. I'll have all of your belongings sent to your address. Stay away from my daughter." He meets my eyes one last time before leading his wife to the nurses' station. Moments later, they're escorted to the back.

I try to blink away my anger as the shock of their reaction rocks through me. Knowing they won't listen or let me explain —or worse, see Piper—has me enraged. Since there's nothing more I can do, I pull my cell from my pocket and call Easton again.

"You can pick me up," I say, defeated.

"Did you get to see Piper?"

"No. Her parents showed up, then fired me."

"What the fuck?"

"I know." I grind my teeth, trying to hold back my emotions. I don't know how I'll ever be able to reach her, and if I do, will I ever see or kiss her again?

"Gimme twenty minutes," he says.

"Thanks, man," I tell him, grabbing the bag the nurse put my prosthesis supplies in.

In record time, my brother arrives and helps me get into the car, then returns the wheelchair inside. Luckily, there's an extra one at the beach house. After I was discharged from the military, my mom wanted to make sure I could visit and never feel immobile. Bless her heart because even though I fought it at first, it's saving my ass today.

"You look like shit," he tells me as he drives out of the parking lot. "So tell me what happened with Jack."

I rehash everything I witnessed and what Piper told me before she was taken away. Then I tell him about my injury and how intense my phantom pains are.

"I don't even care that they fired me, but not to allow me to see her is fucking cruel. They wouldn't even listen to what happened," I mutter, growing more angry as I talk about it.

"Maybe once they cool down and she explains, they'll change their minds," Easton offers.

I shrug, not feeling confident about that. "They're hardheaded. They'll only believe that I failed to protect her, and that's that."

"Man, I'm sorry," he says as he drives on the highway.

"And I have her phone, so she can't call me. If she knew my number by heart, she would've at least tried to get ahold of me. I'm feeling shit outta luck right now," I say, staring out the window.

"Is this where you tell me you're in love with her?"

I turn toward him, and the corner of his lips tilts up.

"I am," I admit. "For the first time in years, I opened up to someone and fell harder than I'd ever imagined was possible. Now it's all over."

"That's not like you to just give up, Tristan."

"I'm being realistic," I counter. "Her parents are too powerful to fight against."

"Have faith, okay? If Piper's feelings are mutual, she'll find a way back to you."

We stay silent the rest of the way, and once we arrive at the house, memories from earlier flood my mind. I have no idea where Jack is, and once we told the EMTs about him, they filed a report with the local authorities. Hopefully, they're keeping an eye out for him or searching for his body. Either way, I'll be looking over my shoulder until there's news about it.

"Do you want me to stay with you a while?" Easton offers after he wheels me inside.

I force a half-smile and shake my head. "Nah, I'd rather be alone." I can hop around and jump up the stairs if I have to. My left leg is pretty strong still, and I don't want to burden anyone.

"Okay. I'm only a phone call away," he reminds me, patting my shoulder as I sit in my wheelchair.

"Thanks."

After Easton leaves, I lock the door, then move around the rooms. Looking at the puzzle on the table, I realize a handful of pieces are still left. I can't bring myself to finish it, though, not without her here. The ghost of her lingers as I close my eyes. This whole situation fucking sucks, and in the end, I lost. I always do.

Two hours pass, and I hear a knock on the door. I can only assume Easton came back since I ignored his phone call an hour ago.

"Go home!" I call out from the couch. He knows how my mind goes into dark places and probably felt guilty for leaving me.

The knocks turn into a repetitive pounding, and I angrily get into the chair, then wheel myself to the door. I speak up as I swing it open. "I told you I wanted to be—"

My words drop off when I see Piper standing in front of me. Her eyes widen when she sees me, and she looks me over from head to toe.

"Baby…"

"Tristan!" She crashes into my chest, wrapping her arms around my shoulders and climbing onto my lap. "Shit, is this hurting you?" She pushes back.

"No, get over here." I pull her against me, crashing my lips to hers as tears stream down her cheeks.

"I was so worried about you," I say between kisses, wiping her cheeks.

"I was worried about you!" she cries out with a laugh.

"How did you…?" I'm in shock that she's here.

"Escape my fucking parents?"

"Yes, and how did you get here? Or find the house even? I'm sorry, I have so many questions right now."

She chuckles, getting off my lap and closing the door behind her. I wheel into the house, then follow her to the living room.

"They left me in the fucking dark. The nurses wouldn't tell me if they treated you and made me wait until my family arrived to tell me anything. I didn't know anyone's number by heart except for Kendall's, so I called her, and she said our parents were on the way. All I could do was wait. When they finally showed up, I told them what happened, and they said they fired you. I was pissed because they didn't even wait to hear the truth. When they insisted I come back to New York with them, I told them no, which of course they didn't like. Then I let them know they can no longer dictate my life. I told them this wasn't your fault. Of course my father is a stubborn jerk sometimes, but I confessed that we were together and that he wasn't gonna stop me from being with you. Once I got discharged, I hugged them goodbye and then called Easton's shop for the address of the beach house. Since we'd talked about it so much, it was easy for me to get the number."

My mouth falls open with amazement. *Holy shit.* "He wasn't there, though."

"Oh, I know. I asked for his cell number and had to beg the woman on the phone to give it to me. Told her it was a family emergency. So, she finally did. Then I called Easton, and he told me a little about what happened."

"Did you drive here?" I ask.

"Hell no. I took a cab. Did you know they have those in Florida too?"

"You're amazing." I chuckle, pulling her back into my lap and kissing her forehead. Her hair smells like the ocean, and I know she's probably exhausted from all the excitement. "I can't believe you did all that for me. I'm so proud of you for sticking up for yourself."

"I can't be without you. I just can't. I know that deep down in my heart, and the thought of never seeing you again because of my asshole dad wasn't something I would just lay down and accept. I know we've only been together for a short time, but you're my other half. I want and need you more than anything. *Even* YouTube," she adds with amusement, and I chuckle.

"I feel the same way. I can't even begin to explain what was going through my mind when your dad fired me and told me to stay away from you. I thought it was the end of us. I was heartbroken."

"Never, Tristan. He can't keep us apart. It's just the beginning."

"What if your parents never approve of us being together?" I ask.

"Unfortunately for them, that's not their decision. It's mine. And I choose you, Tristan. I will always choose you. I love you with every inch of my being."

"I love you so goddamn much. I thought I was going to lose you. I was so worried and didn't know what to do. The thought destroyed me, Piper. The nurses refused to give me updates or let me see you. I was in a full-blown panic."

"You're never going to lose me, Tristan. Never. When I was on that boat and Jack was dragging me away, all I could think about was the possibility of never seeing you again. I promised myself if I survived, I'd tell you how much I love you. Words can't even describe how much."

I brush my lips against hers, knowing exactly what she means. "I thought the same thing, baby. You've changed me for the better, and although it hasn't been that long, it doesn't matter because when you know, you know. I'm in love with you in ways I've never experienced before."

"Tristan," she whispers, searching my eyes. "Prove it."

She follows me to the staircase, and I stand, holding the railings as I hoist myself up each step. Piper continually asks me if I'm okay or if I need help, which I find sweet, but I'm twice her size. If I was at risk of falling, I'd crush her.

Once I'm upstairs, I hop to my bedroom with Piper next to me. "I'm just fine," I reassure her. "I hopped around the apartment all the time at night."

"Just looks painful."

"Nah. My ankle takes a beating, but I'm careful."

As I sit on the bed, I wrap my arms around her and take her down to the mattress with me. She squeals as I bring my mouth to hers.

Moments later, she stands and gives me a little striptease.

"Are those new?" I look at her bra and panties, realizing that's not what she was wearing earlier.

"My parents brought me a change of clothes."

"Ahh," I say, and as soon as I catch sight of her nipple, I wrap my mouth around it.

She runs her fingers through my hair, and her head falls back when I move to the other one.

Slowly, I peel her undergarments off her body. She steps out of her flats and stands naked in front of me.

"So damn gorgeous," I whisper, dragging her between my legs. "I'm so lucky."

"And all yours." Her lips slide against mine, and all I want to do is worship her body the way she deserves. I lift her up until her legs wrap around my waist and she's sitting on my lap.

"Take off your clothes," she demands, tugging at my shirt.

"Not yet," I tell her, then flip her onto her back on the bed.

I lean down, spread her legs, and devour her pussy. Piper grabs the comforter with her fists, writhing against my face as I flick my tongue against her clit. As she grabs her nipples and pinches them, I pull away. Her head pops up, and she gives me a look as I remove my clothes, then settle back onto the mattress.

"Ride my face," I tell her, and she moves into position. With her thighs on each side of my head, she lowers her beautiful pussy down to my mouth. I lick her from top to bottom and listen to her moans.

"Mm, you're close," I say, tasting her juices as she rocks her hips. I tongue fuck her, wanting to drink every drop of her.

"Oh God," she moans as I slide a wet finger into her ass.

"Come on my face, baby," I murmur into the soft skin of her pussy.

"Yes, yes, yes…" Her pace increases as I move my finger in and out of her tight hole. Her thighs tremble, then the orgasm rocks through her body.

"Tristan," she groans. "Tristan." She sounds like she's gasping for air as she rides out the waves of her pleasure. Placing my tongue inside her, she violently throbs.

"I need you inside me." She looks down at me and meets my eyes. I lift a brow. "Now."

"Yes, ma'am. Take my cock, baby. It's yours."

She climbs off and teases the tip with her tongue before licking away the pre-come and placing all of me in her mouth. Going as far down as she can, she nearly chokes on my length, but it doesn't stop her.

In a constant rhythm, she goes up and down my shaft,

causing my eyes to roll in the back of my head. I run my fingers through her hair as she hums and meets my eyes.

"If you keep that up…"

She gives me a devilish grin and inches me closer to the edge. When she notices my muscles tighten, she pulls away and watches my dick twitch. After it's passed, she loops her leg over, then slowly slides down on me until I'm buried inside her.

She topples forward, her mouth crashing against mine as she rocks her hips back and forth.

"I love you," she whispers against my mouth.

"I love you too," I say, gripping her ass, allowing me to go deeper. "So damn much."

"Fuck," she whisper-hisses, her pussy nearly breaking my dick off as she comes for the second time. Piper pushes herself up and throws her head back with a groan. It's sexy and animalistic, and I love when she loses control like this.

"Piper," I whisper between moans. "I'm gonna…" I can barely get the words out.

"Yes, come inside me," she encourages, pounding her perfect pussy against me until the orgasm rips through me. I feel as if I'm floating, having an out-of-body experience as I make love to the woman I want to spend forever with.

She falls against my chest, our breathing ragged as I tightly hold her.

I hold her like she might disappear if I close my eyes.

I hold her like she's mine, and I'm never letting her go—no matter who tries to come between us.

PIPER
ONE WEEK LATER

We stayed at the beach house while we waited for Tristan to get replacement parts for his prosthetic. Since his doctor was local, he could see him right away to get him what he needed. We enjoyed spending quality time together until we had to go back in the public eye, but I have to admit I enjoyed being off the grid with Tristan. While he's had my iPhone the entire time, I told him not to give it back to me until it was safe for me to be online since Jack hasn't been found yet. The temptation to see what people were saying was strong, but I wanted to stay in our bubble as long as possible.

Today is bittersweet because we're flying back to New York this afternoon. We spent the better part of the morning cleaning the beach house and packing. Tristan FaceTimed his parents and formally introduced me as his girlfriend, and I loved the way it sounded coming from his lips. They were shocked and excited, but so nice. I already adore his family so much. The only way I can describe them is genuine and wholesome. His mom invited us to come visit for a week. I told her Tristan taught me how to cook her homemade lasagna, and she almost burst into tears with happiness.

Before we leave for the airport, my burner phone buzzes. I look down and see Kendall's name, so I pick it up.

"Hey, have you left yet?"

"Not yet," I tell her, my heart rate rushing by the tone of her voice.

"Do you have a satellite there?"

"Yes, why?" I ask.

"Turn on the news," she tells me.

I quickly do and see Jack's picture plastered on the screen. "Tristan!" I call out, and he comes over.

"Jack Hall, the known stalker of YouTube star and billionaire heir Piper Montgomery, was found dead this morning during a recovery mission in Southern Florida. Police have been searching for him after he attempted to kidnap and murder her."

Then they show pictures of the capsized boat from a helicopter's view while the news anchors discuss the events that led to his death.

"Wow," I mutter in shock, surprised no one called to tell me before it broke on the news. "I guess that means it's really over."

"It is, baby." He holds me to his chest. "He'll never hurt you again."

"Thanks to you," I remind him, tilting my head up for a kiss. "I'm so relieved. Now I know he's not hiding in the shadows or can plan his retaliation."

"You're safe now."

"I always feel that way when I'm with you," I tell him honestly. "But it's nice to have closure."

"Agreed."

I suck in a deep breath and check the time.

"I guess we should get going soon," he says, and I release him to grab some water from the kitchen.

"Just one more thing," I say, moving to the table and fitting the final few pieces in the puzzle. I can't help but laugh, thinking about how much of a scattered mess it was when we arrived and how it's now complete. Just like my heart.

"Okay, now I'm ready." I smile as he walks over.

"Looks awesome," he says.

"You should have Easton mod podge it for us, then ship it

to New York so we can frame it and put it on the wall. It'll be a sentimental piece."

He wraps his arms around me and kisses my forehead. "I think he'll do anything you ask."

I snicker. "He better. I promised to promote his shop several times, so it's an even trade then."

After we've walked through the house a few times to make sure we haven't forgotten anything, Tristan takes my hand and leads me outside with our luggage. We scheduled a car to take us to the airport, and moments later, it arrives.

As we're boarding the private jet, my nerves get the best of me as I feel like I'm entering society for the first time.

"I guess I'll take my phone back now," I tell him, knowing I'll have to eventually face reality even though I'm dreading it.

He unzips his duffel and hands it over. It feels like a grenade in my hand, ready to explode at any moment. Once we're in our seats, I turn it on but silence the notifications. I put it away, deciding I'll deal with it when I get back to New York, along with my parents and the media. Tristan interlocks his fingers with mine and kisses my knuckles as the plane takes off.

"We'll get through this together," he reminds me.

"Yes, we will."

CHAPTER TWENTY

PIPER

FIVE MONTHS LATER

"I HAVE TO ADMIT, I'm a bit nervous," Tristan tells me as I adjust his tie. He's wearing a suit, one that hugs him in all the right places with a hunter-green tie that brings out his eyes. I'm wearing a dress that matches it with bright red leggings. If Christmas spirit were an outfit, I'd be it.

"Don't be," I reassure him. "My parents adore you."

He gives me a look. "I wouldn't say that, but rather, they *tolerate* me."

"Don't be silly. Mom asks me when we're getting married at least once a week so she can start planning."

He chuckles and runs his fingers through his hair. "So it's official, both of our families want us to get married ASAP and start having kids too." Just like we planned, he moved into my place as soon as we got back to New York, and now everyone's ready for us to get hitched and pop out babies.

"Not just our real-life families but our YouTube family too. All twenty-five million of them. Well, half of them want us to get married. The other half want you all to themselves." I chuckle as his cheeks redden.

"Something about that bodyguard, former military, badass vibe makes them all wet."

His face cracks into a smile. "Is that what you found attractive?"

"You know it," I say as he dips down and gives me a soft kiss. "And sorry, but you're all mine."

"There isn't anyone else in the world I want, babe." His smart watch dings. "Looks like the driver is downstairs. Guess we better get going."

Tristan leads me outside, where a limo is waiting for us. When we get inside, we pour a couple of glasses of champagne and eat strawberries.

Once we arrive at my parents', we see Kendall and Ryan and walk in together.

"Are you ready for this?" I ask. "I just hope they bring out the wine because sometimes they tend to be insufferable during the holidays."

Kendall snickers. "Might be time for me to start volunteering on Christmas Eve and Day too," she says, considering she usually spends every Thanksgiving at the shelter volunteering her time.

"Hey, sis!" Ryan says, pulling me into a side hug, then he gives Tristan a firm handshake.

"How've you been?" Tristan asks.

Ryan explains the hospital has been busy during the holidays with burn injuries and people falling off their roofs putting up Christmas lights.

When we make it to the oversized door, my parents' butler answers and escorts us inside. Charles takes our coats and announces that our parents are in the formal dining room.

The house smells amazing, and I know Chef Jaquel has made a feast of a meal.

Tristan's eyes scan around, and I know he's still trying to adjust to all of this. Hell, a part of me is, too, after leaving the beach house.

There's a twenty-foot Christmas tree in the foyer, and we pass three more as we walk to the far end of the house. It's not the first time Tristan has been here with me, but we don't visit often since I'm usually way too busy with work. Since I got used to having Tristan with me all the time and my father likes the security, he kept him on the payroll as my personal bodyguard. Obviously, I don't mind it, and it gives us the chance to see each other as much as possible. He's a part of my channel now, and it's grown even faster with him being in the vlogs. People love him.

When we enter the formal dining room, the sixteen-person table is full of food. Considering there will only be six of us tonight, it seems like a complete waste, but I put on a smile to appease my parents.

"There are my beautiful girls." My mother sashays over wearing a formal dress with gloves like she's royalty. She kisses each of my cheeks. "Merry Christmas, sweetie."

"You too, Mom."

She gives Tristan a hug, then greets Kendall and Ryan, just as my father comes around the corner with the carving utensils.

"Hope you kids are ready to eat," he says, and I hear a slight tinge of excitement in his voice. "Hey, Tristan. Nice to see you. Ryan," Dad greets. He's smiling wide, something that doesn't happen very often.

"Shall we get started?" Mom waves her arm to the table, and we make our way over.

Tristan looks at me with a smile, and I give him a wink. He pulls out my chair for me, and I scoot in, then he sits beside me.

Dad carves the turkey, and we carefully grab slices off the fancy china. My parents are used to being served every meal, but they usually opt for self-serve on the holidays.

Kendall glances at me, and we hold a small conversation.

"So, are we cracking open the wine, or what?" I finally say.

"Oh yeah!" Mom exclaims and grabs the bottle. The wineglasses are already on the table, and she happily goes around and pours ours. When she gets to Kendall's glass, my sister declines.

I glance at her and tilt my head.

She clears her throat. "I think I have an announcement. Well, we have an announcement to make." Kendall glances at Ryan.

"You're pregnant?" I ask, nearly bursting into tears.

"Yes!"

I stand and run over to her, giving her a hug. "Oh my God, I'm so happy right now. I'm going to be an aunt!"

I bend down and speak to her tummy. "And I'm going to spoil you rotten."

Mom cries, joining the hugs. Tristan stands and pats Ryan on the back, congratulating him. Dad's happier than ever.

"I think cigars are in order," Dad announces.

"After dinner," Mom says, meeting his eyes.

"We just found out, but I knew I had to tell you all tonight. I won't be able to keep it inside much longer." Kendall beams, and I see she's already glowing.

We all return to the table as Kendall continues chatting.

"So, are you hoping for a boy or girl?" I ask.

"Either," she tells me.

"Or both," Ryan says.

Tristan chuckles. "Do twins run in the family?"

"On both sides, actually," Mom responds.

Tristan's eyes widen as the realization we could someday have twins hits him. I chuckle, but I know without a doubt he'd make an amazing father.

Once our plates are piled high, we begin eating.

"Wow, Jaquel did an amazing job on the roasted Brussels sprouts," I say.

"The turkey tastes great," Tristan adds, and everyone agrees.

We eat so much, I feel like I'm going to have to be rolled out of here. The food is to die for, but I guess you're accustomed to it when you have a personal chef.

After dinner, coffee is served, and then Mom brings out the desserts.

"How's work going, Piper?" Dad asks, biting into his slice of lemon meringue.

"Now it's going great. I literally spent the past five months doing damage control after everything that happened."

Reaching over, I grab Tristan's hand, and he kisses my knuckles. "You handled it well, sweetheart."

"Thanks to you." I gaze into his eyes, wishing I could rip off that suit and tie.

"You've been her rock, Tristan. I have no doubt she wouldn't have been able to navigate this without you," my father says, taking us both by surprise.

"Not to mention, your audience is in love with him." Kendall chuckles. "I've read some of the comments. A bunch of thirsty old ladies after your man."

"See!" I look at Tristan as I burst out laughing. "I told you!"

He grunts, still not believing it. He refuses to read the

comments after seeing the mean ones. I've gotten used to ignoring them, but he was ready to murder someone.

"You're a hero," my mom tells him. "Served our country and saved our daughter's life."

"Yeah, he's pretty amazing," I agree. "Plus dealing with everyone in our business."

"It's a lot to get used to," he confirms.

"Absolutely," Kendall says. "It's why I stayed out of the limelight. Too much drama and craziness."

"It's not that bad. Well, now that I have Tristan around to protect me and take some of the spotlight off me," I say.

"You're a good sport," Mom tells him.

"I'll support her no matter what. Even when it gets to be too much, I can handle it," he reassures everyone.

"Sounds like you found a good man," Ryan tells me.

"Well, thank you," Tristan says. After dinner, the men go to Dad's smoking room and light cigars to celebrate the baby announcement. Then Kendall and I stay and chat with Mom as the leftovers are put into containers.

"You both should take some of this home," Mom suggests.

"I would, but we're planning to go see the lights in the city after we leave."

Kendall rubs her belly. "Baby and I will gladly eat it. I hope you two have fun. I miss doing things like that. Ryan's schedule has been so hectic, and I don't particularly like the cold that much."

I snicker. "I know, it's why I'm wearing leggings. They're insulated."

Mom smiles as she meets my eyes. "I really am happy for you and Tristan, Piper. I know we were very hard on you when the death threats started and—"

"Mom, I know," I interrupt her. "No need to keep rehashing it. I love you."

"I love you too and just want the absolute best for you." Mom's already apologized several times for how they treated Tristan. It's something my parents regret, and I'm sure they will probably spend the next few years agonizing about it.

"I just want the best for both of my girls," she adds, pulling me into a hug.

"Aw, I want hugs too," Kendall says and squeezes between us.

"Are you excited to be a grandma?" Kendall asks.

"It's the best Christmas gift I could've asked for," Mom says.

Once the men return, we say our goodbyes, then we leave.

"How was hanging out with my dad and Ryan?" I ask when we're in the car.

He chuckles. "Fine."

"What do three men who don't say very much talk about?"

Tristan wraps his arm around my shoulders and pulls me into him. "You don't even wanna know."

On the way to Times Square, Tristan's phone buzzes in his pocket. He pulls it out and answers a FaceTime call from his parents.

"Merry Christmas!" his dad says.

"Oh my God, are you two dressed up like Mr. and Mrs. Claus?"

Tristan chuckles. "They do this every year. It's their tradition."

"I love it!" I say, then turn to Tristan. "We should start doing that too."

"Absolutely not," he says.

"Hey, bro!" Easton's voice says from behind, and his

parents turn the phone. "How's my favorite future sister doing?"

"Great! As always!" I beam.

"We just wanted to wish you kids a very Merry Christmas!" his mother tells us, and we return the sentiment.

"Wish you were here enjoying this sixty-degree weather," Easton adds.

"Ha, don't rub it in. It's supposed to snow tonight," Tristan tells them.

"Maybe tomorrow you'll wake up to a winter wonderland. How perfect would that be for Christmas!" His mother's voice raises an entire octave.

"That would be amazing!" I squeal. "I love it when that happens."

"What're y'all up to?" Easton asks.

"We're going to check out Times Square and maybe watch people ice skate."

"Yes, it's so fun!" I grin.

"You two have fun!" his parents tell us, and we end the call.

"I love them. They're so sweet," I say as we make our way through the city.

"Forgot to warn you about how extra they are during the holidays. It's bad. They literally dress the flamingos in their yards with Christmas lights and reindeer antlers."

"That's hilarious. We'll have to visit them some year during the holidays," I suggest.

"They'd like that."

"Wouldn't you?" I ask.

"Of course. I don't care where I am as long as you're with me."

Tristan places his palm on my cheek as our tongues twist

together. Things grow more heated, and I'm greedy for him, wanting him right now in the back of this limo. Unfortunately, the car comes to a stop.

"Will you need a ride back to your apartment, Ms. Montgomery?"

"I don't think so. We'll take a cab," I tell him, then thank him for the ride.

"Hope you have a Merry Christmas," he says.

Reaching into my purse, I pull out an envelope and hand it to him. It's a tradition I've had for years because he always drives me around during the holidays instead of spending time with his own family. "You too."

"Thank you, Miss Montgomery." He flashes me a wink.

After Tristan and I get out of the car, he interlocks his fingers with mine and kisses my knuckles.

"I love how generous you are to people," he says, and I shrug.

"Can't bring all this money with me when I'm dead. Might as well make someone else happy," I admit as we make our way through Times Square. It's full of tourists as we squeeze through the crowd.

"You still want to watch the ice-skaters?" he asks.

"Yes, please! It looks so magical with the tree!"

We head that way as he keeps his arm wrapped around me. People snap pictures of us as we walk around, but we pretend we don't see them. I'm sure those photos will be posted online before we get home tonight.

It's ironic because months ago, I would've vlogged this entire evening. Now, it's not even the first thing that comes to mind when we plan things. I'd rather live in the moment with Tristan and enjoy him without sharing every little thing we do with the world. Once we're at Rockefeller Plaza, we turn the corner and take the sidewalk that gives the perfect view of the rink. Wooden constructed angels with golden trumpets line the water. Then I study the large spruce that's full of lights.

I wrap my arms around Tristan's waist as I look up at it. "The rink is on the other side, but I love looking at it from this angle."

"I love looking at you from this angle," he mutters in my ear. In the distance, I can hear Christmas jazz music. Tristan takes my hand, and we dance on the sidewalk. He spins me around, then pulls me in close.

"You know what I was thinking about?"

"What's that?"

He slowly sways.

"Spending the rest of my life with you."

I swallow hard, and my heart pounds in my chest when he carefully gets down on one knee.

I'm confused until I see a black velvet box.

"Piper Montgomery..."

I immediately start crying and don't even let him finish.

"Yes, yes! Oh my God, yes!" I squeal, crashing into him and wrapping my arms around his neck. He holds me as he gets to his feet.

"You didn't even let me finish." He chuckles.

"I'm sorry, I couldn't help it."

Tristan opens the box, then slips the gorgeous diamond ring on my finger.

"You really want to marry me?" I ask.

This is so surreal. I've dreamed about this very moment. And better yet, it's in the most perfect setting.

"I can't imagine my life without you in it. I'm a better person because of you, and I'd be so damn honored if you'd be mine forever. I want to grow old with you and start a family with you. You're my everything, Piper. You've taught me what it is to live again."

My emotions bubble over as I grab both sides of his face and brush my lips gently against his. "You've taught me what it's like to love and be loved. I can't wait to be your wife."

He smiles. "Thank God, baby. Now let's get out of here."

I laugh. "I swear you're a mind reader."

Tristan and I make our way to the corner of the street and hail a cab. It takes everything I can to keep my hands off him on the way back to the apartment, but the last thing we need is to give the driver a show.

"Remember when you asked me earlier what Ryan and your dad and I talked about?"

I nod.

"I asked him for his blessing to marry you."

"You did? What'd he say?"

"Surprisingly, he approved. Said I'm the only man in the world he'd allow you to be with."

Laughter escapes me. I've never been this happy in my life and can't wait for Tristan Belvedere to be my husband. It's a dream come true.

EPILOGUE
TRISTAN

EIGHTEEN MONTHS LATER

"GOOD MORNING," I say, rolling over to greet my beautiful wife.

Her eyes flutter open, and she's wearing a sleepy smile. "Morning."

Next thing I know, Piper is under the blankets, worshiping my cock. I slip my hands behind my head, wondering if this is what royalty feels like. She pumps and works me until I'm nearly ready to explode, then rides me until she almost comes.

I roll her over, steady myself, then take her from behind. As I slam into her, I reach around and rub circles on her clit. I've memorized her body and the way she reacts so well that before she comes, I pull away and tease her just the way she likes. After she finally gives herself permission to come, I follow soon after, and we collapse onto the bed to catch our breaths.

"I'll never get tired of waking up like that," she says.

"Me neither," I admit, grateful for every single day I get to spend with my wife. I think back to what happened while I was in the military and thank the stars every day that I lived. There were points in my life when I wished I'd died that day. Now, I'm grateful I didn't. Deep down, I feel like I survived just so I could meet Piper. She's restored my faith in relationships and reminded me what it's like to be loved.

We got married last July, only seven months after our engagement, and I still haven't gotten used to seeing pictures of our special moment splashed all over the internet. Though I knew exactly what I was getting into, so I couldn't be too mad about it.

Soon, we'll be celebrating our one-year anniversary, but I swear we're still in the honeymoon phase. The wedding was beautiful, extravagant, and expensive—in typical Montgomery fashion. After dealing with her mom being a mother of the bridezilla, Piper was ready to elope but stuck it out because she knew it was important to them too. Our wedding may have beat a world record for how much they spent on it. The only thing I cared about was making sure she was happy and got everything she wanted.

"I want avocado toast for breakfast," Piper says once we crawl out of bed.

I go through the process of putting on my prosthesis, then slip on my shorts. "I think I can make that happen."

While Piper goes to the bathroom to do her morning routine and get dressed, I peel a couple of avocados.

After I toast the bread, I smash the avocado on top, then fry a few eggs.

Just as I'm plating everything, Piper comes around the corner with a camera in her hand.

"And there's my amazing husband making breakfast," she gloats.

I look over my shoulder and grin at how adorable she looks.

"He's mine, ladies. I got the ring to prove it." She giggles as she flashes her left hand, wiggling her fingers. Once she's done talking into the camera, she sets it down.

"Mmm, this smells delicious." She moans, then grabs us some forks and napkins. I pour us two cups of coffee, then join her at the table that oversees the city streets.

"So, what are your plans today?" I ask.

"I was thinking about vlogging some today since I'm only doing weekly updates instead of daily, but other than that, all I need to do is a bathing suit haul."

"Bathing suits?" I arch a brow, not liking the idea of everyone seeing her in teeny bikinis.

"Yeah, Easton sent me a box of swimsuits to try on for a video. The last time I did, they sold out."

"Oh yeah, he told me about that. You're amazing for helping him. I know he appreciates it a lot."

"I love doing it and want him to be successful. It's hard to compete against big corporations, and influencers are expensive as hell to hire. But a little birdy told me people were now begging him for items to share with their audiences," she says with a shrug. "Guess I've started a trend. The hashtag support small shops has *so* many tags now."

I chuckle, amused by how excited she gets. "I love you so much."

"I'll never get tired of hearing that," she admits. "I love you too."

Before she finishes her food, she grabs her camera, then points it at her plate. "Almost forgot to show you the incredible breakfast Tristan made. It was so good, I couldn't wait. Right, babe?"

I smile at her. "You know it."

"How are your subs taking the transition?" I ask.

Once we got married, she decided to post less and change some of her content to be geared toward families. She's been babysitting her nephew, Drew, so Kendall can have a break every once in a while and loves vlogging about him. Of course, people are eating it up because everyone loves babies. Drew just turned one, and when I say they had a freaking circus of animals available for all the infants, I mean it.

Kendall refused to get a nanny and wants to make sure she gives her son tons of love, or at least that's what Piper told me. But Kendall still needs a break once in a while, so we take him when she needs to go shopping or has a doctor's appointment. He's a cute kid and smart for his age. Makes me excited to have children of our own someday.

After we're done eating breakfast, I rinse the dishes. Moments later, Piper comes up behind me and wraps her arms around my waist.

"The beach house remodel is almost finished! It should be ready for when we go next month. Our one-year anniversary is going to be lit."

I chuckle and wipe my hands. "Your choice of words still amuse me."

"Like to keep you young," she says.

My phone rings, and when I see it's Easton, I put him on

speakerphone. I'm sure he's calling to gloat about the skimpy bikinis he sent Piper.

"You're in so much trouble," I tease, and Piper snickers.

"Hey." His voice strains, and we immediately know something's wrong.

"Everything okay?"

"There's been a fire at the shop, and I don't know what I'm going to do. Everything's gone."

Oh my God. That shop was his whole life.

"What do you need?" Piper asks at the same time I say, "What can we do?"

"It's a really long story, but Tatum needs to use the beach house. She's one of my employees who was living in the apartment above the shop. Since we had to evacuate and she needed a place to hide from her abusive ex-husband, I gave her the address and code." His voice shakes, and I can tell he's worked up.

"Hey, man, it's gonna be okay," I try to ease his mind, but I know my words are falling on deaf ears.

"Well since I also need a place to stay until I figure something out, I'll be staying at the beach house too."

"So you're both staying there together?" Piper asks, giving me a knowing look.

"Yeah, I don't feel right leaving Tatum by herself. I have a feeling her ex had something to do with this."

"Why do you think that?" I ask, immediately going into big brother mode. I want to destroy whoever did this, but I know I can't be erratic.

"He came here asking for her, but Tatum told me who he was, so I knew not to say anything. However, I think he figured out I was lying. It's very suspicious how the fire started, and I feel like he was sending a clear message."

Piper covers her mouth with fear in her eyes. Some of this sounds a bit too familiar.

"They'll investigate it," I reassure him. "It'll be easy for them to figure out if it was arson or not."

"Yeah, but hopefully, they don't think I'm the one who did it." He blows out a frustrated breath. "I'm sorry."

"For what?" I ask.

"That I need to use the house. I know Piper's been working on the remodel for the past six months, and you guys are supposed to come here in a couple of weeks for your anniversary."

"Easton," Piper speaks up. "If you need the beach house, then please use it. We have a million other places we can go. Seriously. I'd rather you be safe and have a roof over your heads and focus on your business. Let me know if there's any way we can help because you know I'll send a whole team of contractors to fix it up in a jiffy."

I give her a sweet smile. "Yeah, man. Don't worry about it. If you need an extra set of hands, just call me."

"I appreciate that, guys. I just feel bad about ruining your plans."

"We're more concerned about you than a vacation," Piper states.

"Thank you. Summer is the busiest season, and this is going to hurt us big time." He sighs.

"It's gonna be okay," I offer. "Let the fire chief do his job and then file an insurance claim if you can."

"Yeah, that's the plan."

"Keep us updated, okay?" I tell Easton, and he promises he will.

"Stay safe," Piper tells him, then the call ends.

PIPER

Tristan sucks in a breath, and I can see how upset he is over this. After running his fingers through his hair, he looks at me. "Wow. That sucks so bad, and I hate that I'm not there to be with him."

"I know. I feel so bad for him," I say, feeling awful that he's in this situation. "That's the equivalent of someone deleting my channel and me having to rebuild it. Can't imagine how stressed I'd be."

"Me neither."

"But he did say he was with a woman, and they were going to the beach house together," I offer. "Maybe this is his lucky day in disguise."

Tristan bursts into laughter. "Are you suggesting they're going to fall madly in love just because we did?"

"Yes, it could happen! The house is magical."

He shakes his head as he smiles. "My brother has mentioned her a few times. She's eight years older than him and has only been working there a few months."

"Psshh, like age really matters," I remind him.

He shrugs. "Who knows. They were neighbors and co-workers who probably saw a lot of each other."

"And now they'll be isolated together. Sounds romantic to me," I sing-song.

"When all of this is over, I'm totally going to tell Easton you were shipping him and Tatum."

I clap my hands. "Oh my God, you used it in the right context. Maybe you can teach a millennial new tricks after all."

"Ha! You're gonna pay for that one." Tristan closes the gap between us and tickles under my arms. I scream out our safe word, but he doesn't stop since he knows I'm not in any real pain. I manage to get away from him, but he ends up chasing me to the couch and lands right on top of me. The moment grows still and heated as he crashes his lips against mine.

When we pull away, I meet his eyes and tilt my head. "I have something to tell you."

He nuzzles into my neck, then moves to the shell of my ear. "You want to fuck all day? Because I'd be down for that."

I laugh and shake my head. He pulls away. "Hmm, okay, tell me."

"I'm pregnant," I whisper.

He searches my face. "You are?"

I nod, biting my bottom lip, and he kisses me again.

"You just made me the happiest man in the world. This is surreal."

"I'm so glad to hear you say that because I already went to my first ultrasound, and it's twins."

"You're joking."

"No," I say with laughter. "I swear, I'm being serious."

His eyes widen, then he laughs with me. "Well, you did warn me."

I shrug. "Guess the universe overheard."

"Fine with me. I hope they look just like you."

"They're going to be the perfect mix of both of us," I confirm, so damn excited to go through this journey with him.

I grab his face and kiss him until our lips go numb.

"We're going to be parents."

"We are," I confirm.

"When did you find out?" he asks.

"I realized I was late a few weeks ago and took a pregnancy test. Then another. Then I went to my doctor to be one-thousand-percent sure before I told you," I explain. "I'm so happy, Tristan. I really can't believe this."

"Me too, baby. So damn happy."

Tears begin to spill down my cheeks. "I have all I've ever wanted—you and our babies."

He wipes them away with his thumb and tucks loose strands behind my ear. "This is a dream come true, Piper. Thank you. Thank you for loving me and making me a father."

"You know, that night of the boat accident, I feared for our lives, thinking you'd been shot and killed, and I was going to drown to death. And look, now we're starting a whole new chapter." My emotions get the best of me while I finish my sentence.

"Yes, sweetheart. Forever and always." He kisses me again. "God, I love you so damn much."

I nod, laughing. "I'm blaming these happy tears on pregnancy hormones."

He chuckles. "We have so much to look forward to and new things to experience together."

"We do. And I can't wait to share this with the world, but only when you're ready to announce it."

"I'll let you make that decision. I trust you to make the right call."

I sigh, but I can't stop grinning. "Why are you so perfect?"

"Because I finally have what I've been missing all of my life—*you*." Tristan bends down and lifts my shirt, then kisses my belly. "And you too, little ones."

Curious about what happens with Easton and Tatum? Find out next in *The Heart of Us*

WHAT'S NEXT

Next in the Love in Isolation series is Easton & Tatum story in _The Heart of Us_

What happens when you're on the run from your psycho ex-husband and your sexy younger boss goes into hiding with you to keep you safe? You slowly remember what it's like to fall in love and hope he feels it too.

The Heart of Us is an older woman/younger man age gap, close proximity standalone romance.

AUTHOR'S NOTE

Dear reader,

Thank you so much for picking up *The End of Us*! We hope you enjoyed Tristan and Piper's story as much as we enjoyed writing it. For several years, I've wanted to write a hero who was an amputee since I have a personal experience with being married to one and didn't see much representation of them in romance books. I was hesitant for a while, but knew Tristan was the right man for it. (-Brooke)

Tristan's case with being an amputee is quite common, although it varies from person to person. Most amputees struggle with chronic phantom pains, emotional trauma, and mental health issues. Though we could've dug deeper into his past and what he went through, we wanted to focus on his life after recovery and how it still affects him years later. The reality of being an amputee comes with lifelong struggles and we wanted to show just some parts of what those could be.

The loss of Tristan's brothers impacted him immensely, especially after the other survivor passed away so shortly after they returned home. It helped him realize a gap in veteran's mental health awareness in the military—an average of 22 veterans commit suicide each day in the United States and over forty percent of veterans struggle with mental illness. You can read more information about 22 Suicides a Day here: https://tadsaw.org/22-suicides-a-day/

If you're interested in donating to wounded vets or reading more about The Wounded Warrior Project, read about it here: https://www.woundedwarriorproject.org/

Thank you again for reading!
-Brooke & Lyra AKA Kennedy Fox

ABOUT THE AUTHOR

Brooke Cumberland and Lyra Parish are a duo of romance authors who teamed up under the *USA Today* pseudonym, Kennedy Fox. They share a love of Hallmark movies, overpriced coffee, and making TikToks. When they aren't bonding over romantic comedies, they like to brainstorm new book ideas. One day in 2016, they decided to collaborate under a pseudonym and have some fun creating new characters that'll make you blush and your heart melt. Happily ever afters guaranteed!

CONNECT WITH US

Find us on our website:

kennedyfoxbooks.com

Subscribe to our newsletter:

kennedyfoxbooks.com/newsletter

- facebook.com/kennedyfoxbooks
- twitter.com/kennedyfoxbooks
- instagram.com/kennedyfoxduo
- amazon.com/author/kennedyfoxbooks
- goodreads.com/kennedyfox
- bookbub.com/authors/kennedy-fox

BOOKS BY KENNEDY FOX

DUET SERIES (BEST READ IN ORDER)

CHECKMATE DUET SERIES

ROOMMATE DUET SERIES

LAWTON RIDGE DUET SERIES

MOCKINGBIRD DUET

INTERCONNECTED STAND-ALONES

MAKE ME SERIES

BISHOP BROTHERS SERIES

CIRCLE B RANCH SERIES

LOVE IN ISOLATION SERIES

TEXAS HEAT SERIES

ONLY ONE SERIES

Find the entire Kennedy Fox reading order at
Kennedyfoxbooks.com/reading-order

Made in the USA
Monee, IL
06 October 2022

15351911R00136